Isabella likes

CRUSH

Does he like her too?

Isabella's Spring Break Crush
by Angela Darling

D1502853

SIMON SPOTLIGHT
New York   London   Toronto   Sydney   New Delhi

SIMON SPOTLIGHT
An imprint of Simon & Schuster Children's Publishing Division
1230 Avenue of the Americas, New York, New York 10020
Copyright © 2014 by Simon & Schuster, Inc.
Text by Ellie O'Ryan
Designed by Dan Potash
All rights reserved, including the right of reproduction in whole or in part in any form.
SIMON SPOTLIGHT and colophon are registered trademarks of Simon & Schuster, Inc.
For information about special discounts for bulk purchases, please contact Simon & Schuster Special Sales at 1-866-506-1949 or business@simonandschuster.com.
Manufactured in the United States of America 0114 OFF
First Edition 10 9 8 7 6 5 4 3 2 1
ISBN 978-1-4814-0493-8 (pbk)
ISBN 978-1-4814-0494-5 (hc)
ISBN 978-1-4814-0495-2 (eBook)
Library of Congress Control Number 2013941963

chapter 1

ISABELLA CLARK POKED AT HER SALAD WITH A plastic fork. Normally she loved talking with her friends at lunchtime, but today it was just making her depressed.

"And our resort has its own private beach," her friend Amanda was saying. She was practically jumping up and down in her seat as she talked. "So we can just walk out of the hotel and right onto the beach. And the temperature there right now is eighty degrees! Isn't that awesome? I am so tired of the cold."

"And the snow," added Jasmine, glancing toward the nearby window. Mounds of winter snow were piled up in the middle school parking lot and along the walkway. Icicles dripped from the bare tree branches. Snowflake flurries swirled around in the freezing wind.

"It's Chicago. It's supposed to be cold in winter," Isabella said, repeating something her dad said often. It never really made her feel better to hear it, though. She loved the summer, when she didn't have to bundle up every day. The summer sun just made everything feel happier.

"Well, I *love* the snow," said Lilly. With her white-blond hair and blue eyes, Lilly always appeared to Isabella as some kind of snow princess from a fairy tale. "I can't believe we're finally going skiing in Colorado! It's going to be awesome."

Jasmine frowned. "We're not going far at all. Mom's taking us to the Buffalo Lodge. It's kind of lame, but at least they have an indoor pool."

Amanda turned to Isabella. "So, are you guys doing anything?"

Isabella sighed. "You know we never do. My dad says this year I can help out in his office and make some extra money."

"That's pretty lame too," Lilly remarked, and Amanda shot her a look. "I don't mean that Bella's lame. I mean her dad is lame, you know, for making her work."

"It's okay," Isabella replied glumly. "You're right. It is lame."

"It's not all that bad," Amanda said, trying to cheer

her up. "That way you can buy those great earrings we saw at Sparks."

"Yeah," Isabella said, and then she started poking at her salad again. Amanda was supersweet and a great best friend. But nothing she said could get Isabella out of her mood.

It just wasn't fair! She was pretty sure that her family was the only one in the whole school who didn't go anywhere during spring break. Things got complicated for the Clarks during this time of year.

For one thing, even though it was "spring break," it still felt like winter in Chicago. Isabella's mom was a pediatrician, and this time of year she was bombarded with kids coming down with the flu.

And it's not like her dad could take them anywhere. Mr. Clark was an accountant, which meant he had to help dozens of people do their taxes before April fifteenth. So he couldn't leave his job either.

"We'll make it up to you in the summer," her mom always said, and it was true—they always went on a nice vacation in the summer. But their last vacation was a distant memory now, and in two weeks all she had to look forward to was filing folders in her dad's office as she watched the snow fall outside.

"Well, the week goes by fast anyway," said Amanda.

Jasmine was scrolling on her phone. "Hey, I forgot that Buffalo Lodge has horseback riding! Maybe it won't be so bad after all."

Lilly leaned in and lowered her voice. "Okay. If you could go on spring break with any boy in our class, who would it be?"

"That's easy. Colin Hancock," Jasmine replied. "He's so cute."

"No way!" Lilly squealed. "I was going to pick him!"

"Well, I think I would want to go with Brian Bender," Amanda said a little shyly.

"Him? He's so nerdy!" Jasmine said.

"That's why I like him," Amanda replied.

Lilly turned to Isabella. "What about you?"

Isabella shrugged. "I don't really know." Which was true. She had never had a real crush on a boy yet. Sure, there were some nice, cute boys in her class, but she would never think of, like, *dating* any of them. "Besides, it doesn't matter, because I'm not going on spring break anyway."

Finally, the lunch bell rang. Isabella was glad the

conversation was over, but she still couldn't stop thinking about break.

I'll keep working on Mom and Dad, she plotted as she gathered up her books for her afternoon classes. *There has to be some way to save spring break!*

She waited until dinner that night. It was a Thursday night, which meant that Mom got home late so Dad made spaghetti and heated up meatballs from the freezer. Isabella's job was to make a salad. Her twin brother, Jake, was in charge of garlic bread, and they both had to set the table.

Isabella found a pot of water heating up on the stove when she came into the kitchen to make the salad. Her dad was infamous for starting things in the kitchen and then wandering off to make a phone call or check something on his computer. Isabella's mom got so mad at him when he did it. She always said he was going to burn down the house. Usually everyone yelled at him when he did it, but tonight Isabella just took the big yellow salad bowl out of the cabinet and then got vegetables out of the refrigerator and put them on the counter. Next she got out the box grater so she could shred the carrots into the salad just the way her dad liked. Normally she just chopped them up because she was always a little afraid of using the grater.

Jake came into the kitchen while she was grating the carrots. He stopped.

"So what are you asking Dad for?" he asked.

Isabella wasn't surprised that Jake knew she had ulterior motives for grating the carrots. It was one of those twin things. It wasn't like they could read each other's minds or anything, but sometimes she knew what Jake was going to say before he said it, and vice versa—stuff like that. Or she could usually tell just by looking at Jake if he was worried about something, or keeping a secret, or coming down with a cold.

Isabella looked around. Parents had a way of popping up behind you when you least expected them.

"I really want us to go on spring break," Isabella replied.

Jake nodded. "Me too. But you know we can't go."

"But there's got to be some way," Isabella pointed out. "Mom can't be the only doctor in Chicago who treats the flu. She could find someone to fill in for her."

"Yeah, well, what about Dad?" Jake asked.

"He could have a working vacation," Isabella reasoned.

"He does half of his work here on his computer anyway."

Jake picked up a carrot and bit into it. "Might work. Go for it."

That's Jake, Isabella thought, *just happy to go with the flow*. If she hadn't brought up spring break, he wouldn't have asked. That's just the way he was.

Sometimes it was hard for her to believe that they were twins. Sure, they both had fair skin, hair that couldn't decide if it was brown or blond, and green eyes. And they both had what their parents called "the Clark nose," which turned up a little bit at the end and which every Clark was supposedly born with.

But Isabella was about a half an inch taller than Jake (although Dad pointed out that boys grow more slowly than girls). And Jake's green eyes had a hint of blue in them while Isabella's had a hint of brown, but only when it rained.

Anyway, lots of brothers and sisters looked alike, not just twins. But their personalities—that's where they were really different, Isabella thought. Jake was always really . . . mellow. Things didn't bug him. He took everything in stride. If his pillow was lumpy, he would sleep on it without complaining.

Isabella was the opposite. If something bugged her, she wanted—no, *had*—to fix it. If she had a lumpy pillow, she wouldn't sleep a wink until she found a pillow without lumps.

"If life were an ocean, Jake would be riding the currents and Isabella would be on a Jet Ski, speeding past him," their mom said once. And the funny thing was, Isabella was sure that Mom was complimenting her, but Jake was sure he was the one being complimented. Mom said that meant they were each happy with who they were, and that was good.

Isabella noticed steam pouring from under the lid of the pot on the stove, and she picked up the lid and peeked inside.

"Dad, you're boiling!" she yelled.

Mr. Clark came rushing in, tucking his phone into his front shirt pocket. He picked up a box of spaghetti from the counter and dumped it into the boiling water.

"Thanks, Isabella," he said. "Oh gosh! I forgot to do the meatballs. Guess I'll microwave them. Mom will be home soon."

Isabella finished the salad at the same time that Jake got done slathering butter on the bread and sprinkling it with garlic powder.

"Dad, can you turn on the broiler?" Jake asked.

"Sure thing," Mr. Clark said.

Then Isabella took the utensils out of the drawer while Jake took plates out of the cabinet.

"That's five," Isabella corrected him. "We only need four, remember?"

"Oh, yeah," Jake said casually, taking away a plate, but Isabella saw a cloud briefly pass over his face. The fifth plate would have been for their older brother, David, who had gone away to college that fall. Isabella missed him, but she knew Jake missed him even more.

Fifteen minutes later, the table was set and topped with the salad, garlic bread, and spaghetti and meatballs right at the moment their mom walked into the door. Mr. Clark high-fived Isabella and Jake.

"We are a well-oiled machine," he said.

"Smells great in here!" Dr. Clark said, peeling off her hat, coat, scarf, and gloves. Underneath it all was a tall woman with sandy blond hair like the twins and a perfectly fine nose (even though it wasn't a "Clark nose").

Isabella's mom washed her hands at the sink ("Hand washing is the enemy of germs!" was her motto) and then they all sat down at the table. They chatted for a few minutes about the usual stuff—what happened in school, the client who brought Mr. Clark chocolate chip cookies, the patient of Dr. Clark's who stuck a marble up his nose. Then there was a break, and Isabella saw her chance.

"So, I've been thinking. It's not too late for us to plan a trip for spring break," she said. "In fact, I saw some great last-minute deals online."

Dr. Clark sighed. "Oh, honey, I know how much you want a break, but you know that your dad and I have to work."

"I was thinking about that," Isabella said, and then she launched into the plan that she had told Jake. "So it's definitely possible, right?" she finished.

"You know that you two have to be careful in the sun because of your fair skin," Dr. Clark said.

"You know we're always careful when we go out in the sun," Isabella countered. "And anyway, I'd be happy just to get away. We don't have to go to a beach. There's lots we could do."

Here Mom and Dad looked at each other. Isabella wished she could read their faces the same way she could read Jake's, but her parents were a different story.

"We'll think about it," her mom said, and Isabella

didn't push it. But her mind was racing as she finished her dinner.

After she and Jake cleared the table, Isabella headed up to her room, taking two steps at a time. She opened her laptop and started searching the Web.

Best spring break destinations, she typed, and pictures of palm trees and white beaches popped up on her screen. Everything looked amazing. She took notes about the ones that seemed the best, like a hiking trip out West and a scuba-diving vacation in the Caribbean. She even took down the info on Buffalo Lodge, just in case her parents didn't want to go too far.

But she knew a great destination alone wouldn't be enough to sway her parents.

Benefits of vacation, she typed, and she was excited to see links to tons of articles appear—and some of them were written by doctors. Her mom would love that.

She read a few of them, taking a lot of notes. One of them said that people who take vacations got sick less often and were less stressed out. Another one said that people who go on vacation were more productive at work. Her dad would love that one.

She started to work on a presentation on her computer

when her dad knocked on the door.

"You're awfully quiet in here. Homework?" he asked.

"No, a special project," Isabella answered.

"Well, good for you," said Mr. Clark. "But you need to wrap it up and get ready for bed, okay, hon?"

"Sure, Dad," Isabella said. She didn't need the presentation anyway. She would slay them with her amazing facts!

That night, as Isabella slept, a wind howled outside the window, painting it with frost. But she didn't hear it. She was deep inside a dream, sitting under an umbrella on a white sandy beach, listening to the sound of gentle waves lapping against the shore.

chapter 2

ISABELLA WAS PREPARED WITH HER PITCH WHEN her family sat down to dinner the next night.

"I have two charts here," she said, patting a yellow folder next to her dinner plate. "One is a list of possible spring break vacation spots, listed in order from closest to Chicago to farthest away. The second chart has a list of all of the proven benefits of taking a vacation. Did you know that it can lower your blood pressure?"

Next to her, Jake rolled his eyes, but she ignored him. As she reached for the folder, her dad held up a hand.

"You can distribute those after dinner, Isabella," he said. "I don't want to get gravy all over them after you've worked so hard."

"And I appreciate your research, Isabella, but your dad and I already told you we'd think about it," her mom said.

"That's why I made the charts. To help you think," Isabella replied.

Her mom smiled and shook her head. "You are my little steamroller sometimes. I promise we'll give them a good look, okay?"

Isabella nodded. She knew her mother meant it.

"Oh, and I forgot one thing," Isabella added. "David posted online that *he's* going on spring break. So I think it's only fair that all of us get to go."

"That's different," her dad said. "David has been working in the college bookstore and saving his money so he can go away with the baseball team. He's an adult now."

"But we will take that under consideration," added her mom. Isabella had heard her use that phrase before. It was one step better than "no" and slightly better than "we'll see."

"On one condition," her mother added, rubbing her head. "No more charts, please. In fact, no more talking about spring break. We'll give you a decision soon."

Isabella frowned. She knew her mother meant that too. One more peep out of her about spring break and her mom would toss the idea out the window.

To her surprise, Jake came to her defense. "What

about me? Can I ask you guys about spring break? Because I think it's actually a pretty good idea."

Isabella gave her brother a grateful smile.

"No. That rule goes for both of you," their mom said, smiling brightly. "Okay, then. Who wants to tell me about their day at school?"

Not talking about spring break in the house was a hard bargain for Isabella to keep. That night they all watched a movie together on TV, and a commercial for the Bahamas came on. She almost blurted out, "That's number seven on my chart!" but she stopped herself.

The next day was Saturday, and Lilly invited her and Amanda over to hang out. It was another cold, slushy day, and Isabella was glad to have a reason to get out of the house. She played flute in the middle school band, but those practices were after school, not on weekends. And soccer season wouldn't start until after spring break.

"I definitely have the winter blahs," she announced as Lilly opened the door for her.

"Yay! Bella's here!" Lilly cried, pulling Isabella inside. "Amanda's already upstairs. Take off your coat!"

"Hold on. I've got to get my boots off too," Isabella said.

She stuffed her hat and gloves into her pockets and slid off her coat, which Lilly grabbed. Then she sat down and pulled off her boots, lining them up with the other boots in the Millers' front hallway.

She and Lilly bounded upstairs to Lilly's bedroom. Amanda was sitting on Lilly's bed, surrounded by piles of clothes.

"Did your closet explode?" Isabella asked.

Lilly laughed. "No. I'm packing!"

She picked up a fluffy white sweater and held it in front of her. "Won't this be perfect for the ski lodge? I have a pair of skinny jeans in here that will go great with it. And wait until you see the new ski outfit my mom got me."

She rummaged through the clothes on the bed and pulled out a pair of light blue ski pants and a matching jacket with white trim.

"Isn't it cute?" she asked.

"It matches your eyes," Isabella said, feeling a pang of jealousy. She was happy for her friend, but part of her wished that she were going on an awesome trip with a new wardrobe too.

"Lilly, you're not leaving until next week," Amanda pointed out.

"It's never too early to pack!" Lilly shot back. "Ooh, show Bella that picture of the new bathing suit cover-up you got. It's sooooo cute!"

Amanda looked at Isabella as if to say, "Do you really want me to?" *She knows what I'm thinking*, Isabella realized. *That's why she's my best friend!*

Isabella nodded. "It's okay. I want to see it."

Amanda found the picture on her phone and passed it to Isabella. A model with sun-kissed hair was wearing the cover-up, and it really was cute—white with yellow vertical stripes, a halter-style top, and a short skirt.

"Oh, wow. I can totally see you in it," Isabella said. "You're going to look great. And you're going to have a great time."

"I wish you could come with me," Amanda said.

"Me too," Isabella said with a sigh.

Later, when her mom picked her up, Dr. Clark asked Isabella, "So, what did you girls do today?"

Free pass! Isabella realized. Now she could talk about spring break without breaking her mom's rule.

"Lilly was packing for her spring break skiing trip," Isabella said. "And Amanda showed me a picture of this cute beach cover-up she got for her trip."

Dr. Clark raised an eyebrow. "Oh, really?"

Isabella just nodded, afraid to say anything more. "Um-hmm."

For the rest of the weekend, Isabella was on pins and needles. She kept hoping her mom or dad would bring up the subject of spring break, but neither of them said a word. By Monday, as Isabella stepped out into another cold, dark Chicago morning, she was starting to feel hopeless. Friday was the last day of school before break. If her parents didn't plan a trip soon, it would probably be too late.

That night at dinner, she was poking a fork into her pork chop when her mom made a show of clearing her throat. Isabella looked up from her plate.

"I have an announcement to make," her mom said, and a surge of hope rose in Isabella. "You guys could do well with a change of scenery. It's been a long winter, and Dad and I are going to be very busy in the next week. So . . ."

She looked at Isabella and Jake, beaming. Isabella couldn't contain her excitement. Her mind raced through the suggestions she had made on her chart. Were they going to Hawaii? Snorkeling in the Caribbean?

"The two of you are going to visit Grandma Miriam in Florida!" Dr. Clark finished.

Isabella stared at her mom in stunned silence. Jake looked pretty stunned too. *Grandma Miriam?*

Isabella felt her hopes for a great spring break crash and burn. She loved Grandma Miriam a lot. She was funny, and she loved David, Isabella, and Jake like crazy. But "Grandma Miriam" and "vacation" were two things that just didn't go well together.

They had visited Grandma Miriam in Florida before, and it was Boring with a capital B. For one thing, Grandma Miriam always got up early—like crazy early, before even the birds were up—so she could swim laps in the pool in her condo complex.

In fact, she never seemed to stop moving, and she was always making the kids exercise even if they didn't feel like it. She thought it was wrong to watch TV during the day ("That's what sick people do!"), and she didn't have anything in the house with sugar in it ("Raisins are nature's candy!").

And when she wasn't swimming or stretching or mall walking, she loved to sit around and talk. And talk. And talk. Which Isabella always thought was nice for the first hour or so, but then she would get bored and want to go on the Internet. She was usually able to slip away and get on her phone because Mom and Dad were there to talk to Grandma Miriam. But this time, it would be just her and Jake.

She turned to Jake with a look of desperation, but her brother looked excited and happy.

"Cool!" he said. "We get to fly by ourselves?"

Dr. Clark nodded. "Your dad and I have talked it over and we feel that you are both very responsible. You're old enough and we trust you. You'll have a flight attendant helping you, and Grandma Miriam will be on the other end to meet you as soon as the plane lands."

A flight attendant helping us? How embarrassing! Isabella thought.

"This is going to be awesome," Jake said. "We can go in the pool every day!"

"But only during certain hours," Isabella reminded him. "Remember? They don't let kids in it for half the day so the old people can swim in peace."

Jake ignored her comment. "Maybe she'll take us to the alligator farm again. And remember that time we went to the batting cages?" He kept babbling on about how great the trip was going to be.

Isabella wasn't so sure. This was *so* not what she'd planned. No scuba diving, or snorkeling, or adventures. There was a beach near Grandma Miriam's, but she only let them go in the early morning or late in the afternoon so they would miss the strongest rays of the sun. It didn't matter how much sunscreen Isabella promised to wear or how big their beach umbrella was. Grandma wouldn't budge.

"I won't have the skin of my beautiful grandchildren being fried!" she would yell.

"Bella?" Dr. Clark asked. "Aren't you happy? You got your wish!"

As if, Isabella thought, but she didn't want to sound ungrateful. "Sure. It sounds good," she said.

"You should thank your mom, Bella," her dad said. "I thought it would be good to have you earn some spending money by working in my office, but she wanted you kids to enjoy yourselves while your old parents will be working like dogs."

Isabella felt a little guilty. Her mom had been looking really tired lately. It seemed like every night she was getting calls from parents with sick kids. And her dad had been going into the office extra early, even before she left for school, so he could come home and make dinner for them. And then after dinner he would have to work.

She flashed her mom a smile. "Thanks, Mom!" she said, and she hoped she sounded like she meant it.

She broke the news to her friends the next day at lunch.

"So, my parents are sending Jake and me away for spring break," she said.

"Oh, I'm so happy for you!" Amanda squealed. "Where are you going?"

"To my grandma's," Isabella replied.

"The one who lives in DC?" Lilly asked.

Isabella shook her head. "No, the one who lives in Florida."

"That's good, right?" Amanda asked. "You'll be near the beach. And it will be warm. Lots of Florida sunshine."

"Only Grandma won't let me go out in the sun," Isabella complained. "Or watch TV during the day. It's going to be so boring!"

"Well, maybe she'll let you and Jake do some things by yourselves," Amanda said, always looking on the bright side.

Isabella tried to imagine Grandma Miriam letting them out of her sight.

"I don't think so," she said with a sigh. "But I guess it's better than staying here."

"Definitely!" Amanda said. "Just think, you'll be leaving the snow and the cold behind. No more dressing like the Abominable Snowman!"

Isabella laughed. It was hard to be in a bad mood when Amanda was around.

"Promise you'll text me," Isabella said.

Amanda grinned. "Of course!"

That night, the phone rang at Isabella's house, and she picked it up.

"HAVE YOU HEARD?"

Isabella knew the loud voice on the other end immediately. It was Grandma Miriam. She talked LOUDLY. ALL. THE. TIME. Mom said it was because she didn't hear well anymore, but Dad said she was always loud.

"Hi, Grandma," Isabella said. "Yes, I heard."

"I'm so excited!" Grandma Miriam said. "What a treat to spend a week with two of my beautiful grandchildren. I have so many fun things planned for us, Izzy. You won't be bored for a second!"

Isabella couldn't help smiling. Hearing Grandma

Miriam's voice reminded her of how much she missed her. Her grandmother was the only one who called her Izzy, and she didn't mind. It made her feel special.

"I know, Grandma," Isabella said. "I can't wait!"

"And you're not going to believe this," Grandma Miriam said. "But you and Jake won't be the only kids here. Rose's grandson, Ryan, will be here, and you can all go to the pool together!"

Isabella's excitement faded. She had met her grandma's friend Rose before, and, boy, was she annoying! She complained about everything all the time and seemed like she was about two hundred years older than Grandma Miriam. Her grandmother was always busy swimming laps or going to museums or one of the discussion groups they had at the clubhouse in her condo complex. But Rose didn't ever seem to leave the house. Grandma Miriam said she was just shy.

Isabella tried to imagine what a grandson of Rose's would be like. Probably short and pale with glasses, and he would probably be complaining every minute, just like Rose.

Jake and I will get stuck babysitting him and carting him around wherever we go, she thought. *Ugh.*

This is getting worse by the second!

"Oh, wow," Isabella said in a flat voice. "I can't wait to meet him."

"I'm sure you'll love him!" Grandma Miriam said. "Now, go put your brother on the phone. I don't want him to think I'm playing favorites."

Isabella found Jake and handed him the phone. "It's Grandma," she said, and then she headed into her room.

Might as well think about packing, she thought, opening the drawer in her dresser where she kept her summer clothes. Her mom wouldn't take her shopping; she was too busy, and anyway, what was the point? She'd only be going to Grandma's. She started pulling out some T-shirts and shorts.

Jake came bounding into the room. "Isn't this going to be so great?" he asked.

Isabella was tired of pretending in front of Mom and Dad. "Uh, no," she said, and Jake's eyes got wide. "My idea of a vacation is not going to see Grandma Miriam and hanging out at the old people's pool and getting stuck hanging out with her loser friend Rose's grandson."

"Bella, you have a bad attitude," Jake said. "We get to go hang out and have fun, and Grandma Miriam spoils us rotten. It's going to be great. At least my vacation is. I hope yours is too."

He stomped out of the room.

SPOILS us? thought Isabella. *Grandma's idea of a treat is a box of raisins. How is that being spoiled?*

chapter 3

"KEEP YOUR CELL PHONE ON UNTIL THEY MAKE you turn it off on the plane," Dr. Clark was saying. "I want to make sure I can contact you, all right?"

"Sure, Mom," Isabella said with a yawn. It was 6:17 in the morning, but you wouldn't know it inside the busy terminal at O'Hare International Airport. Travelers scrambled around them in every direction under the terminal's bright fluorescent lights.

"You're all checked in," Mom went on. "We're almost at security. I won't be able to go through with you, but there will be a flight attendant there who will take you to your gate."

"We got this," Jake said confidently. He looked wide awake.

Dr. Clark hugged them both supertightly. "I will miss you two! Be good for Grandma, okay?"

"Of course," Isabella said grumpily. *What were they, five?*

The twins had to pry their mom off them when they got to the security line. As they got to the check-point, a woman in a blue uniform approached them, smiling.

"Isabella and Jake Clark?" she asked.

"That's us!" Jake replied.

"I'm Jeni. I'll be taking you to the boarding area," she said.

Mom waved and looked like she didn't know if she should leave or stay.

"We're good, Mom!" said Jake, and Mom grinned.

"I'll just wait a few minutes more!" said Mom, and Isabella rolled her eyes.

They followed Jeni to the moving sidewalk, which took them down a long corridor with glass walls. Outside, Isabella could see the planes docked at the gates. The sidewalk ended and opened up into a wide room with more glass windows. There were five different boarding areas, each one with a desk and seats for the waiting passengers.

Jeni pointed to an area marked B-7. "That's your gate. You two are old enough to walk around a bit if you want. Just meet me there in a half hour, and don't leave this terminal, okay?"

Relieved that Jeni wouldn't have to babysit them, Isabella and Jake readily agreed.

"So, what should we do?" Isabella asked her brother.

"Walk around, I guess," Jake said with a shrug.

Right by the boarding gates was a row of shops and food stands, so they headed there. They hadn't gone far when Isabella heard the text tone on her phone. It was from her mom.

Did u guys get to the gate OK?

YES! Isabella replied.

K. Let me know when u board.

K.

Isabella shook her head. "It's like she thinks we're little kids."

"Forget about it," Jake said. "I'm gonna get some fries."

"At six thirty in the morning?" Isabella asked.

"It's never too early for fries," Jake replied.

He led her to one of the food stands and ordered his fries. Isabella's phone beeped again.

Did u pack ur sunscreen? her mom texted.

2 bottles! Isabella replied.

Her mom texted back a smiley face, but Isabella didn't feel like smiling. *This annoying vacation is getting more annoying*, she thought. She reached over and grabbed one of Jake's fries, and they walked around the terminal.

Isabella stopped at a gate for a flight to Los Angeles. "Imagine if we were going there? We could see the Hollywood Walk of Fame and probably meet celebrities and stuff."

"Boring," Jake said. He walked over to the big digital display that showed all the flights in the airport. To make the best of it, she and Jake took a walk around the terminal pretending they were going to the different places listed at each gate.

"Look, we could go to Guam," Jake said, pointing.

"Why Guam?" Isabella asked. "You don't even know what it's like there."

Jake shrugged. "It sounds cool."

"How about Tokyo?" Isabella asked, pointing to another one.

"Hmm, I want a flight to New York," Jake said. "So I can visit the Baseball Hall of Fame."

"Los Angeles would be way better," Isabella argued, but they were having fun.

Before they knew it, it was time to get back to the gate. Jeni was waiting for them.

"Right on time," she said. "You guys get to board first."

That wasn't as cool as it sounded, Isabella thought. She felt like everyone was looking at them as Jeni led them to their seats—one by the window and the one in between the window and the aisle seat.

"Can I have the window?" Isabella asked, knowing that her easygoing brother would oblige, and he did.

They settled into their seats. Isabella was about to open the magazine she had brought with her when her phone beeped.

U board yet? her mom texted.

Just did! Isabella replied.

Thankfully, the announcement to turn off all electronic devices came a few minutes later. Isabella looked out the window as the plane sped down the runway and then slowly lifted into the air. As they flew across Chicago, she could see the houses and other buildings below them. Then the houses got smaller and smaller and all she could see were white, fluffy clouds.

After the plane was flying steadily, Jeni came around with the beverage cart. The businessman in the aisle seat next to Jake ordered a coffee. Isabella ordered a water.

"I'll have two sodas, please," Jake told Jeni, and Isabella's eyebrows went up.

"Mom would freak out if she knew you were drinking soda," she said.

"Mom's not here," Jake said casually, taking the two cans that Jeni handed him.

"Okay, but why two?" Isabella asked.

He smiled, handed her one, and then held up his can. "Cheers!"

They tapped cans. "To a great spring break!" Jake said.

Isabella smiled back. *This is probably as good as it's going to get*, she thought.

Two and a half hours later, they landed in Tampa International Airport. Jeni walked them back to the security area, and on the other side, they could see Grandma Miriam waiting for them.

Grandma Miriam was their mom's mother, so she'd probably had sandy brown hair at one time, but now it was streaked with gray. She had on a big, floppy orange hat and wore an orange and white striped shirt, white shorts, and orange sandals with a big flower on top of each foot.

"Yoo-hoo!" she was yelling, and she was waving her arms like crazy.

The twins thanked Jeni and then ran to their grandmother, hugging her. They hadn't seen her since last Thanksgiving and it felt like such a long time.

Grandma Miriam stood back and looked at them. "You two you are growing so much!" she gushed. "I have all sorts of things planned. The day is young!"

Oh boy, thought Isabella. *Here we go!*

"So I made us some sandwiches for lunch," Grandma

Miriam was saying. "Then I thought we could go to the orange grove. It's very shady there under the trees. Then we'll go to the pizza place for dinner and go for a walk, and I rented a movie for us."

"You mean we can order one on TV?" Jake asked.

Grandma looked confused. "Who does that? I went to the library and got a video for us! You're going to love it."

Jake and Isabella exchanged glances. They were both hoping that it wasn't some dumb kiddie movie. But they didn't want to spoil Grandma's mood; she seemed so proud of herself.

They went from the airport to her condo complex, a small, tidy community with two-story town houses made of sandy stone. Each house had a tiny front lawn with palm trees in front. Grandma's house was right down the street from the clubhouse and the pool.

Since it was just Jake and Isabella, they each got to have their own room. Grandma put Isabella in the guest room with the white wicker bed and matching dresser. The bedspread had a pattern of colorful tropical flowers.

"Now, you two unpack, and I'll set up lunch," Grandma told them.

As Isabella placed her clothes in the drawers, she

marveled at how sunny and warm it was here and how pretty the room was. A vacationy feeling was creeping up on her, whether she liked it or not.

When she got to the kitchen, her grandmother was hanging up her phone.

"That was your mother," Grandma Miriam said. "She wanted to make sure we all got here safely."

Isabella shook her head. "She worries too much!"

"That's what mothers do," Grandma Miriam said, and she smiled as Jake bounded into the kitchen. "Let's eat!"

Grandma Miriam hadn't lost an ounce of energy since Thanksgiving. After lunch they helped her clear the table, and then they drove to the orange grove. Grandma produced three white umbrellas from the trunk of her car.

"Grandma, it's not going to rain," Isabella said.

"These aren't for the rain. They're for the sun!" she said loudly, thrusting one into Isabella's hand. Isabella opened it, feeling a little silly, but she had to admit that it worked.

They took a tour of the orange grove, which was interesting but seemed to take hours. Then they went to the grocery store to pick out cereal for the week and, oddly, Grandma didn't object when Jake grabbed a big box of chocolate-flavored cereal. Then they went to an Italian restaurant for pizza, and when Jake asked if they could get ice cream for dessert, Grandma Miriam said yes!

"Really?" Isabella asked.

"Oh, well, your mom isn't here," Grandma said with a wink. "I try to follow her rules, but this week we follow my rules. And I love dessert."

Who are you, and what have you done with Grandma Miriam? Isabella wondered.

They went back to the condo, and Grandma held up a DVD case.

"It's movie time!" she said. "I got *The Sound of Music*! Can you believe nobody else took it out?"

Jake couldn't help making a face. *"The Sound of Music?"*

"Don't tell me you've never seen it!" Grandma sounded shocked. "I need to scold your mother about that. Good thing it's never too late."

Isabella had never heard of it either. It turned out to be a musical about a family with a lot of kids who lived in Germany during the Second World War. They had no mom, just a dad and a nanny, and the nanny taught them how to sing. So they gave a concert for the German soldiers and escaped while they were singing.

Isabella would have thought that a movie set in such a serious time would be sad, but it ended up being really interesting and even fun. Grandma Miriam knew all the words to all the songs and sang along really loudly to each one. She and Jake started giggling, which made her sing even louder.

By the time the movie was over, Isabella was exhausted. She barely had the energy to shower and get into her pajamas. As she was settling into bed, Grandma Miriam came in to say good night.

"Did you have a good time today, my beautiful Izzy?" Grandma asked.

"Yes," Isabella said, and she meant it. The day had been really fun.

"Just wait until tomorrow," Grandma said. "Rose's grandson, Ryan, will be going to the pool with you. Isn't that nice?"

"Um, sure," Isabella said, but she was lying. They were just starting to have fun with Grandma, and now they would be stuck hanging out with some annoying kid!

chapter 4

"RISE AND SHINE, IZZY!"

Isabella groaned and opened her eyes. Florida sunshine streamed through the window, thanks to Grandma Miriam pulling up the blinds. Her grandmother's hair was wet, and she wore a white terry-cloth swimsuit cover-up.

Isabella glanced at the clock.

"Grandma, it's only eight o'clock!" she complained, pulling the pillow over her head.

"Only eight o'clock? I've been up for hours," her grandmother replied. "I already swam my laps and I've got breakfast cooking downstairs. So get out of bed, lazybones. Your brother is already dressed."

That figures, Isabella thought. She felt like she could sleep for four more hours. Grandma Miriam might have relaxed some of the rules, but it looked like she was still a fan of waking up early.

Her grandmother left the room, and Isabella sleepily got dressed in a pair of denim shorts and her soccer T-shirt from last season. Looking into the mirror on the white wicker dresser, she could see her sandy hair was a tousled mess, but she didn't feel like brushing it. She pulled it back into a scrunchie and headed downstairs.

The delicious smell of bacon hit her nose before she even got into the kitchen, and Isabella suddenly realized how hungry she was.

"There she is!" said Grandma Miriam with a big smile. "I made pancakes and bacon. Turkey bacon, because it's better for you."

"I don't care what it is; it smells great," Jake said. He was already seated at Grandma's square kitchen table, piling his plate high. Grandma Miriam looked delighted.

"Oh, I have missed cooking for teenagers," she said. "The way you eat! It's wonderful. You'll both be six feet tall before the summer's over."

Isabella giggled. "I'd have to buy a whole new wardrobe," she said. "Hey, maybe that wouldn't be so bad."

She took a seat across from Jake, and Grandma fixed herself a cup of coffee at the counter.

"So, I can't wait for you two to meet Ryan," she said. "He's such a lovely boy!"

Isabella rolled her eyes at Jake. He scowled at her and shook his head.

"Where does he live?" Jake asked.

"He lives in New York," Grandma replied.

"In the city?" asked Isabella. *That would be kind of cool.*

"Yes," Grandma replied, sitting down between them at the table. "He lives in the city with his mother and father. He's an only child."

Isabella thought about that. The twins' brother, David, was six years older than they were. Mom and Dad had thought they'd have only one child, but they'd changed their minds and then had Jake and Isabella. Mom was an only child, and since she'd been lonely a lot, she wanted David to have a sister or a brother.

"And," she always liked to say, "I gave him both!"

Isabella liked hanging out with Jake. At home they were always running to different activities or hanging out with their friends, so they didn't spend a ton of time together anymore, not like when they were little kids. But when they were together, it was nice to have someone to talk to, someone who understood her. Jake wasn't one of those annoying brothers; he was actually pretty nice and funny. When they did hang out, they had fun together. They didn't need a third wheel.

Is Ryan lonely? Isabella wondered. She could imagine him as a loner with no friends, and that's why they had to hang out with him.

"But we won't be seeing him until after lunch," Grandma Miriam continued. "No kids in the pool until one o'clock, I'm afraid."

"So what are we doing this morning?" Isabella asked.

"Well, actually, I thought you two might want to chill out for a little while," Grandma Miriam said, stunning Isabella once again. "We did have a busy day yesterday."

"Seriously?" Isabella asked.

"Sure, read a book or do whatever it is you do with your phones," Grandma said. "Unless you want to go out somewhere."

"No, that's okay!" Isabella and Jake said at once. The idea of "chilling out" sounded pretty good to both of them. Isabella read a book and played with an app on her phone, and before she knew it, Grandma was feeding them egg salad sandwiches. Then she and Jake put on their bathing suits and followed Grandma over to Rose's town house.

Isabella had put her shorts and T-shirt on over her bathing suit, and the sun was hot on her bare (except for sunscreen) arms and legs. Grandma Miriam led them through the narrow, winding roads of the condo community. All of the town houses looked the same to Isabella, and she wondered how anyone could tell them apart. One summer when they'd come to visit, Isabella had gotten really lost with David when they were riding bikes. David had to use the GPS on his phone to get back.

Grandma walked faster than both of the twins, and Isabella had a hard time keeping up in her flip-flops. Finally, Grandma turned down the walkway of one of the town houses. Isabella could see that the curtains were closed tightly.

Rose's apartment was always dark; that was one thing Isabella remembered. Grandma Miriam would say, "Rose, open the blinds and let some light in!"

"The heat!" Rose would reply, and then Grandma would say, "That's what the air-conditioning is for! Turn it up!" But Rose would wave her hand and complain that it was too expensive.

Grandma knocked on the door, and they waited . . . and waited.

"She isn't moving too well these days," Grandma whispered—although her "whisper" was as loud as a normal person's voice.

I hope Rose didn't hear that, Isabella thought.

Finally, Rose flung open the door.

"There you are!" she cried. "Oh, so much bigger than last time! They grow so fast!"

Isabella gave Rose a kiss on the cheek. She always smelled like roses.

Rose smells like roses. Ha! That's funny. I never thought of that before, Isabella realized.

"Come, come meet my Ryan!" said Rose, as she started walking toward the kitchen. "I have some nice lemonade, and I made some muffins. Ryan loves my blueberry muffins."

At the word "muffins," Jake hurried after Rose. Isabella held back a little bit, peeking past her into the kitchen.

There, sitting at the kitchen table, was possibly the cutest boy she had ever seen. Cuter than any of the boys in middle school—even Colin Hancock, whom all of her friends seemed to have a crush on. His hair was brown and a little bit in his face, and he had the nicest smile she had ever seen.

For some reason, Isabella was suddenly concerned about how she looked—her faded T-shirt, her messy hair pulled up. It was too late to do anything about that now, but she reached into her pocket and pulled out the tube of lip gloss she always carried with her.

She quickly turned around and applied the lip gloss. Then she saw Grandma Miriam smiling at her—and then she winked. How. Totally. Embarrassing.

"Chapped lips," Isabella said, and Grandma's grin got bigger. She stepped past Isabella.

"Ryan, these are my grandchildren Isabella and Jake. They came to visit their old grandma," she said.

"Nice to meet you," said Ryan a little shyly.

"Ryan, stand up when you meet someone!" Rose scolded, shaking her head. "Ugh, the manners on these kids!"

Ryan turned red, and Isabella knew how he felt. Grandma Miriam wasn't the only embarrassing grandmother in the world.

"Hi, Ryan," said Jake, shaking his hand.

Isabella gave a little wave. "Hi!"

"Let's have some lemonade," Grandma Miriam

suggested. "And some of your famous muffins. Then we can let these kids go have some fun at the pool."

Wait, Grandma Miriam was letting them go to the pool by themselves? Isabella and Jake shared a look, and Grandma caught it.

"Don't worry. I'll check up on you every forty-five minutes to make sure you're reapplying your sunscreen," she said with a twinkle in her eye.

Isabella shook her head, and she and Jake sat down at the table. Jake took a seat next to Ryan, and Isabella was kind of relieved about that. She suddenly felt shy and weird.

Is this what it's like to have a crush? she wondered. Then she brushed the thought away. How could she have a crush on someone she just met?

"So you're on spring break too?" Jake asked.

"Yeah," Ryan replied. "Well . . ."

"Ach, tell them. There's nothing to be ashamed of!" Rose prodded.

"Well, I thought I'd be on a traveling baseball team, but I didn't make the draft, so my parents sent me—I mean let me—come down here so I wouldn't sit at home and, well, sulk, I guess," he explained.

"That's too bad," Jake said sympathetically. "Maybe

you can make it next year. I know baseball is really competitive at our school."

Isabella wondered where Jake had learned to be so friendly. Her parents always joked that Jake could make conversation with anyone. Her mother loved to tell how when Jake was a toddler, it used to take them twice as long to do errands because Jake would be stopping to talk to everyone. Why wasn't she that way? They were twins, after all.

Ryan nodded at Jake. "It's crazy! I mean, people hire private coaches and everything. I tried my best, but . . . maybe next year is right." He seemed to be a little more at ease just talking about it. Jake had that effect on most people, Isabella thought.

"Now, besides the sunscreen, let's go over some rules about the pool," Grandma Miriam said. "No running or shoving each other. But you three are mature enough that I shouldn't have to tell you that. Stay under the umbrella when you're not swimming. And watch out for Mr. Stern at the pool. He's the one with the radio next to his chair, and his skin is orange. He gets cranky when kids are at the pool, so whatever you do, don't splash him."

"He's orange?" asked Jake.

"Don't ask," said Rose. "He looks terrible." Then she turned to Ryan. "Do you have sunscreen on? And not that SPF 15 stuff. The stuff I bought you yesterday."

"I'm all set, Grandma," Ryan promised.

Rose shuffled to the kitchen counter and grabbed a tote bag, which she thrust into Ryan's hands. "There are chips and fruit and some bottles of water."

"Thank you!" the twins said together.

"No cookies?" asked Grandma.

"Of course cookies," replied Rose. "Chocolate chip. I made them special."

"Well, I might share those with Jake and Isabella," Ryan said with a mischievous grin.

Rose laughed and waved them out. "Be back by four thirty for dinner!"

"Sure, Grandma," Ryan said. "We have to leave the pool at four anyway. No kids after four. Remember from yesterday?"

As soon as they got out of the house, they started laughing. "Man, dinner at four thirty," said Ryan, shaking his head.

"It's crazy," agreed Jake. "But our grandma gets up at like five a.m., so I guess that's dinnertime for her."

"I know," said Ryan. "I tried to sleep in this morning,

and at seven thirty my grandmother kept poking me and asking if I was sick."

"Wow, and I thought Grandma Miriam was bad for waking me up at eight," Isabella said.

Ryan grinned. "Lucky!"

Ryan knew the way to the pool, which was pretty big and almost always empty—except for one man with a fake tan, lying on a lounge chair listening to a radio.

"That must be Mr. Stern," Isabella whispered. "He really is orange!"

"Let's go over there," Ryan said, pointing to the opposite side of the pool.

They set up their stuff on three lounge chairs under a big umbrella. Jake and Ryan quickly peeled off their T-shirts and Isabella did the same. Her bathing suit from last year was a blue one-piece racing suit that was faded on the sides. She suddenly wished she had put on the new suit her mom had bought her.

"Last one in is a rotten egg!" shouted Jake, and he bounded into the pool.

Maybe it was a twin thing, but Isabella could never ignore a challenge from her brother. She forgot about her faded bathing suit and ran to the deep end and jumped in one step ahead of Ryan.

"Gross!" she cried, as she crested the top of the water. "It's so warm!"

Ryan laughed. "They keep it at, like, ninety degrees!" he said.

Isabella started paddling around on her back. It might be warm, but it was still a pool. Ryan swam up next to her.

"So you guys are twins?" he asked.

Isabella nodded.

"Who's older?" he asked.

Jake made a face, because he hated when anyone asked this question. Isabella loved it.

"Me!" she cried. "By nine whole minutes."

"That's because you're so pushy," Jake teased, splashing her.

"You kids stop that splashing!" Mr. Stern yelled from his lounge chair.

"Yes, sir!" Jake called out politely, but when he turned back to Isabella and Ryan, he was laughing like crazy. He climbed out of the pool and took a beach ball out of the duffel bag he'd brought with him. Then he jumped back into the pool.

"Let's play pool ball!" he announced.

"What's pool ball?" Ryan asked.

"You make up the rules as you go," Jake explained. He tossed up the ball and batted with it both hands. It soared across the pool and landed in the shallow end.

"Two points!" he cried.

Ryan swam and grabbed the ball. "My turn!"

They played pool ball for a while, until Jake yelled, "Pool ball is making me hungry!" Then they climbed out, dried off, and had some of the snacks Rose had packed.

"We'd better put on our sunblock again, under penalty of death from the grandmas."

They had the spray-on kind that comes in a tall can. Isabella and Jake had a routine since they were little kids. After spraying the front of their bodies, Isabella would spray Jake's back and then Jake would spray Isabella's. When they were done, Ryan handed his can to Isabella.

"Hey, could you do my back, please?"

"Uh, sure," Isabella said, blushing. It was no big deal, really, spraying somebody's back. But the whole time, she couldn't help thinking how *cute* Ryan's back was. Was that possible? Could somebody have a cute back? She was almost relieved when she finished.

"All set," she said, handing the can back to him. Then she stretched out on a lounge chair.

"Good idea," Jake said, and he and Ryan joined her.

"It feels really good to be out of school," Ryan said.

"Definitely," Isabella agreed.

"School's okay," said Jake. "My history teacher is so funny. He, like, acted out the whole Battle of Gettysburg for us with sound effects and everything."

"I like science class best," Isabella remarked.

"Me too!" Ryan said. "Biology, mostly, but chemistry's fun too."

"Definitely," agreed Isabella.

"If you ever come to New York, you should go to the Hall of Science," Ryan said. "The exhibits there are amazing."

"Well, we have the Museum of Science and Industry in Chicago," Isabella said. "They just had this whole special exhibit where you could see animals from the inside out. It was gross but totally fascinating at the same time."

"You guys are geeking out on me," Jake said, jumping back in the pool.

The afternoon seemed to fly by to Isabella. They talked, swam, and snacked some more, and before she knew it, it was time to go back to the grandmas. Jake and Isabella walked Ryan back to Rose's.

"See you tomorrow," Ryan said with a wave, and Isabella felt her heart skip a beat. *He wants to see me tomorrow!*

"I like him!" Jake remarked as they walked to Grandma's apartment.

"Yeah, he's pretty nice," agreed Isabella. *More than just pretty nice*, she thought. But she certainly wasn't going to tell that to Jake.

As they approached Grandma Miriam's, they noticed a woman staring at them through the front window of the town house next door. She had bright red hair and bright red lipstick.

"Did you have a good time?" Grandma Miriam asked.

"Yes," Isabella replied. "Grandma, who is that woman next door? She was staring at us."

Grandma Miriam shook her head. "Oh, that's Lorraine Shelby. She moved in six months ago. She gets involved in everything that goes on around here. Now, why don't you two shower and change, and I'll take you out to eat?"

They quickly obeyed, and she took them to a restaurant on the water. They got a table outside and ordered seafood platters piled with shrimp and fish and clams. As they ate, they watched boats pull up to the dock with fresh fish.

The air smelled salty and warm, and Isabella loved the feel of it on her skin.

"Why do we live in Chicago?" she moaned. "It's so cold there!"

"That's what I say!" Grandma said, reaching over to hug her. "Move down here and be closer to me!"

That night, Isabella was exhausted once again. Her mom had texted her about twenty times, and she answered each one. Then she remembered she had to text Amanda. She sent her a picture she'd taken of Ryan and Jake at the pool.

He's so cute! Amanda texted. No cute boys here.☹

He's nice 2, Isabella replied.

U like him! Amanda said.

Maybe! Isabella said. So how is the beach?

She wasn't ready to admit she had a crush on Ryan. But she was pretty sure that's what it was. She couldn't stop thinking about his laugh, his smile. . . .

Is he thinking about me too? she wondered. *And what if he isn't? What happens when you have a crush on somebody and they don't like you back?*

She turned off her phone and snuggled under the covers. This spring break was turning out to be a lot more interesting than she'd anticipated!

"GUESS WHAT, IZZY," GRANDMA SAID AS SHE opened up Isabella's blinds the next morning. "We're going to a museum this morning with Ryan."

Isabella sat up in bed a little faster than she had the day before. "Really?" she asked with a yawn.

"Rose called me and said Ryan suggested it," she said. "He said you would like it, Izzy. Isn't that sweet?"

"Sure," Isabella said, and she knew she was blushing. It *was* sweet. Did that mean Ryan liked her back? She thought about texting Amanda. She really needed some advice on this stuff.

"We're leaving soon," Grandma Miriam said. "So please get dressed and I'll see you downstairs."

Isabella sighed. She'd have to text Amanda later. This time, she brushed her hair and put on her lip gloss. Then she looked through her drawers, hoping to find something cute to wear, even though she knew she hadn't brought anything. She settled for another pair of denim cutoffs and a pink T-shirt with a cupcake on it that she'd had since she was, like, ten.

Grandma had cereal, toast, and cantaloupe for them for breakfast, and after they brushed their teeth, they drove over to Rose's to get Ryan. Isabella was in the passenger seat, so Ryan climbed into the back with Jake. Isabella noticed that he had brushed his wavy hair; it wasn't as messy as it had been yesterday. Did he do that for her?

Ryan leaned over the front seat, smiling.

"It's not a science museum, but it looks like they have cool history stuff there, so I thought maybe both you guys would like it," he said.

"It's one of my favorites," Grandma Miriam said. "That was a nice suggestion, Ryan."

"Yeah, thanks," Isabella said, smiling back at him.

The museum was all about the history of Florida, including the Tocobaga people who had lived in the area before the settlers came. There were maps and dioramas showing what things had looked like long ago and artifacts from the Tocobaga culture. Isabella's favorites were the pottery pieces, which had really cool designs carved into them.

"The pottery is my favorite too," Grandma Miriam agreed. "I loved doing pottery with my students back when I was an art teacher."

"I totally forgot you used to teach art!" Isabella remarked. "That must have been fun."

Grandma nodded. "I miss my students sometimes."

"You should teach an art class at the clubhouse," Ryan suggested. "I bet lots of people would come."

Grandma Miriam's face lit up. "What a wonderful idea! I'm surprised I didn't think of it before." She gave Ryan a squeeze. "What a smart boy you are, Ryan. No wonder Rose talks about you all the time."

Ryan blushed in a way that Isabella thought was absolutely, positively adorable. She was dying to take a picture with her phone, but that would have been too awkward.

After the museum, Grandma took them to a food truck that sold gourmet tacos. Isabella got one stuffed with chicken, avocados, and mango salsa, and she was secretly pleased when Ryan ordered the same one. During the whole lunch, everyone was talking and laughing like they had known one another forever. Ryan was so easy to talk to! And he seemed to like Isabella as much as she liked him.

Maybe having a crush isn't so hard, Isabella was thinking. *You like somebody nice; they like you back. Simple!*

"Do you three want to go back to the pool this afternoon?" Grandma asked.

"Yes!" they all replied at once, and everyone started laughing.

Grandma drove back to the condo complex and dropped off Ryan. "I'll change and meet you guys over there," he said, and Isabella swore he was looking right at her.

"We won't be long," she promised, feeling excited. This was shaping up to be a totally perfect day!

But when they parked in Grandma's driveway, there was a surprise waiting for them. Lorraine Shelby, Grandma's next-door neighbor, was standing outside with two kids who looked like they were Isabella and Ryan's age. In fact, it looked like they were twins too!

"That Lorraine is so competitive," Grandma Miriam muttered under her breath, and Isabella wondered what she meant. When they got out of the car, Lorraine walked over. She was a lot faster than Rose, Isabella saw, and almost as fast as Grandma.

"Miriam, we've been looking for you!" she said. "You know Andrew and Ashley, my beautiful grandchildren. They live right over in Orange Grove, so I said, why not come visit your grandmother for a few days? Even though they just came for a visit last month." She looked right at Grandma Miriam when she said that, and Isabella could tell that she was bragging.

Andrew and Ashley stared at her and Jake from under mops of sun-kissed blond hair. Isabella thought they looked a lot more alike than she and Jake did. They also happened to look like fashion models, with perfect features and even more perfect tans. Ashley had a fancy manicure with sparkly gems on her nails and a pedicure to match.

"So, we'll see you at the pool later," Ashley said.

"Uh, yeah, sure," Isabella replied, but her hopes for a perfect day were fading fast. She, Ryan, and Jake had formed a comfortable trio. What would it mean now that these two perfect twins were in the mix?

It didn't take too long to find out. When Jake and Isabella got to the pool, Ashley and Andrew were already there. They had towels, flip-flops, and snacks strewn all over a bunch of lounge chairs. Ryan raised his eyebrows when he saw Isabella, as if to say, "Who are these guys?"

Isabella gave a shrug, and Jake jumped into the pool, as usual. "Last one in is a rotten egg!" he said.

The splash made by five kids jumping into the pool was too much for Mr. Stern.

"You kids watch it!" he yelled, and then he turned up his radio really loud.

Jake grabbed the beach ball. "Let's play pool ball! You make up the rules as you go along."

Andrew jumped in front of Jake and took the ball from him. "Steal! Five points!" he yelled. Then he tossed the ball to Isabella. "Heads up!"

It soared over her head, and he swam up to her, splashing. "You missed!"

"Hey, quit it!" Isabella cried, splashing him back. Playing pool ball was no fun with Andrew, so she climbed out of the pool and stretched out into the lounge chair next to Ryan's and closed her eyes.

"So you're from Chicago, right?"

She opened her eyes and saw Andrew was sitting next to her—in Ryan's chair!

"Yes," Isabella replied flatly.

"That's cool. I've never been there. But it's in one of my favorite video games, *Street Race 9*. Did you ever play it?"

Isabella shook her head. "I'm not really into video games."

"No way!" Andrew cried. "That's crazy." And then he proceeded to describe all of his favorite games to her.

Isabella kept glancing over at the pool. Jake, Ryan, and Ashley were playing pool ball the right way, having fun and laughing. She felt a little jealous.

"Okay, well, I'm going back in the pool," Isabella interrupted him.

"Yeah!" Andrew agreed, and he got up when she did.

Isabella swam over to the deep end. Maybe if she did laps, Andrew would leave her alone. She swam past Ashley and the boys, trying to hear what they were saying.

"Yeah, I can't believe they traded him," Ashley was saying, and Ryan and Jake were nodding. "That was totally lame."

She's talking baseball, Isabella realized. That wasn't one of her favorite sports. When she swam back past them again, Ashley was still talking. These twins really liked to talk.

"Snack time!" Jake yelled, and they all piled out of the pool and sat around one of the tables.

"So, Ryan, I was thinking about that one artifact we saw," Isabella began, but Andrew butted in.

"Did you guys go to the history museum? That place is mostly boring, but there are some cool things there. This one time . . ."

Andrew talked so much that it was impossible to have a conversation with Ryan. Isabella was relieved when four o'clock came around, until Andrew said, "We'll walk you guys home. We're neighbors, right?"

"We should walk Ryan home first," Isabella said.

"That's okay," Ryan said. "I can walk home by myself. See ya."

"Later!" Ashley called after him.

Jake and Ashley walked ahead of Isabella and Andrew, talking and laughing. Andrew kept asking Isabella questions about Chicago that she found totally annoying.

"How am I supposed to know the speed limit on the highway there?" she snapped. "I don't even drive."

When they reached Grandma's town house, Isabella practically ran inside. She showered and changed and then helped Grandma set the table for dinner.

"I hope you don't mind my chicken cutlets," she said, putting down a platter in front of them. "I know it's not restaurant food."

"It's better than that. It's Grandma food," Jake said, and Grandma Miriam beamed at him.

"So, how was the pool?" she asked.

"Okay," Isabella said listlessly.

Jake turned to Isabella. "He so likes you."

She thought he meant Ryan liked her, and she blushed. "He does not."

"Are you crazy? It's so obvious that Andrew likes you."

Isabella was shocked. "Oh, I thought you meant—you think so? I thought he was just being obnoxious."

"Well, those twins have a lot of . . . personality," Grandma Miriam said tactfully.

"I kind of liked it better when it was just the three of us," Isabella admitted.

Jake shrugged. "They're fine. I don't mind them."

They finished dinner, and as they were cleaning up, there was a knock on the door.

Maybe it's Ryan, Isabella thought, her heart taking a leap. But when she opened the door, the Shelby twins were standing there. Andrew was holding a bowl of popcorn, and Ashley held a DVD case.

"It's movie night!" Andrew said, and the two of them walked past her into the condo.

Grandma Miriam looked a little perturbed. "Well, I suppose if you want to watch a movie . . ."

"Gran said you wouldn't mind," Ashley said. "She has a headache."

"Then of course," Grandma said. "Make yourselves at home here."

Andrew obeyed immediately, flopping down on the couch and planting the popcorn bowl on the coffee table.

Isabella had an idea. "Um, we should invite Ryan," she suggested.

"He's doing something with his grandmother," Andrew said quickly.

"Oh, he didn't mention that," Isabella said, but she didn't want to make a big deal out of it. Then everyone would know she had a crush on Ryan.

She sat down on the opposite end of the couch from Andrew, and he scooted over to sit next to her.

"You're gonna love this movie," he said.

Jake took the DVD case from Ashley. "Awesome!" he said. "I heard the car chases in this are amazing."

Jake popped the movie into the DVD player. It was one of those action movies about guys who rob banks. There were a lot of car chases and bullets flying. Not Isabella's favorite kind of movie, for sure, but the other kids seemed to be having a good time. In fact, Jake had moved next to Ashley on the floor, and they were both making comments the whole time and cracking up.

A weird thought popped into Isabella's head. *Did Jake have a crush on Ashley? Or did Ashley have a crush on Jake?* It was strange imagining her twin having a crush on anybody.

When the movie ended, everybody got up and stretched. Ashley grabbed the DVD and the empty popcorn bowl, and she and Andrew headed for the front door.

"Well, thanks for the double date!" she said, and Andrew gave Isabella this huge grin. She was mortified.

Grandma Miriam, who had been out of the room during the movie, had come in to say good-bye to the twins.

"There's only one person old enough in this room to be dating, and that's me!" she said, and Isabella was grateful. The thought of dating anybody—even Ryan—was pretty scary.

"Well, that was interesting," Isabella said when the

door had closed behind the Shelby twins.

"Yeah, great night," Jake said.

Grandma Miriam gave Isabella a sympathetic look. Isabella responded with a hug.

"What's that for?" Grandma Miriam asked.

"Just because," Isabella said, because what she was feeling was hard to put into words.

It was just nice to have a grandma who understood!

chapter 6

"I WONDER WHO'S CALLING SO LATE," GRANDMA Miriam said as the phone rang. "Izzy, can you pick it up? It must be your mother."

But the voice on the other end belonged to Ryan.

"Hey," he said. "My grandma asked me to call you guys to see if you want to go to dinner with us tomorrow night."

Isabella's heart jumped a little. "That sounds great. Let me ask Grandma Miriam."

She quickly asked her grandmother and got back on the phone.

"She says yes!" Isabella reported. Then she giggled. "So, four thirty, right?"

"Of course," Ryan said. "I tried to make it six, but she thought I was crazy."

"So, sorry you couldn't come over for the movie tonight," Isabella said.

"What movie?" Ryan asked.

Isabella wasn't expecting that. "Um, it's just that . . . we watched a movie tonight, and we um . . . heard you couldn't make it."

"That's weird," Ryan said. "Who told you that?"

Isabella didn't want to hurt Ryan's feelings, and she especially didn't want him to know that they had been hanging out with the Shelby twins without him.

"I, um, I forget," she said. "It was kind of a dumb movie anyway. So I'll see you tomorrow?"

"Yeah, sure," Ryan said, and they both hung up.

Isabella gave a relieved sigh. The Shelby twins might have ruined everything today, but tomorrow they were going out to dinner with Ryan!

The next morning, Isabella took out every single item of clothing she had brought with her and spread them out on top of her bed. She didn't have anything to wear for a nice dinner out. Her pink shorts had a stain on the front pocket, and her T-shirts all looked blah and boring. She wanted to look nice for her dinner.

And not just because it's with Ryan, she told herself.

I don't want Grandma to be embarrassed if we go somewhere nice!

She picked up her cell phone and called her mom, who picked up on the first ring.

"Hey, Bella," she said. "I'm between patients. Everything okay?"

"Yeah, it's fine," Isabella replied. "It's just that . . . I was wondering if I could use that credit card you gave us for emergencies."

"Is there an emergency?" Dr. Clark asked, sounding a little panicked.

"Well, more like a fashion emergency," Isabella replied. "I just brought a bunch of old clothes with me, and we're going out to dinner tonight with Rose and her grandson, and . . ."

"Rose's grandson is there? How nice. He's the same age as you and Jake, isn't he?"

"Yeah," Isabella replied. "There's a bunch of kids here, actually. Anyway, could I use the card to get some clothes?"

"Hmm. Please put Grandma on the phone," her mom said.

Isabella went downstairs and found her grandmother

in the kitchen, drinking coffee and reading the newspaper.

"Mom wants to talk to you," Isabella said, handing her the phone.

Grandma took the phone. "Good morning, love," she said, and then Isabella could tell she was listening. Grandma got up from the table and walked over by the refrigerator. Isabella's right foot busily tip-tapped on the floor as she waited to hear the answer.

Finally, Grandma walked back to her, smiling. "Looks like we're going shopping," she said.

Jake walked into the room. "I am *not* going to the mall," he protested.

Grandma frowned for a moment, but then her face brightened. "Let me call Rose," she said. She dialed the phone. "Rose? It's Miriam. Yes, I know, it's going to be another hot one today. Could Jake spend the morning with Ryan? I need to take Isabella to the mall."

Isabella felt a pang of regret, thinking how much fun she could have had spending the morning with Ryan. But she quickly pushed the feeling away. Grandma had taken her shopping before, and it had been really fun.

"Let me put on my walking shoes," Grandma said, looking down at her sandals.

A half hour later, they were walking through the entrance of the air-conditioned mall.

"So where do you want to get these clothes? Should we go to Hamilton's?" Grandma Miriam asked.

Hamilton's was a big department store that Grandma loved to shop in, Isabella knew. But the clothes for girls her age weren't exactly cute.

"Um, could we go to Sparks?" Isabella asked. "That's the store Mom always takes me to."

"Of course! This is your day, Izzy," Grandma said. She marched over to the mall directory. "Now, let's see. . . . Here we go. Second floor!"

At the top of the escalator they saw the purple, glittery sign for Sparks right in front of them. The store was packed with racks of cute summer clothes in bright colors. Pop music blared from speakers inside the store.

Isabella practically ran inside. She made a beeline for the first thing that caught her eye: an adorable white, lacy, sleeveless sundress with a sewed-in fake leather belt around the waist. Isabella took it off the rack and held it up to herself.

"What do you think?" she asked.

"Beautiful!" Grandma said. "But you should try it on."

"Of course," Isabella replied. This was why she loved shopping with Grandma. When she went with her mother, it could be stressful. She thought everything Isabella picked out was "too tight" or "too short" or "not appropriate."

The next thing she saw was the swim cover-up that Amanda had picked out. It was the same style, but this one was pale blue with green stripes.

"So cute!" Isabella said.

"That looks pretty skimpy for a dress," Grandma said.

"It's to wear over your swimsuit," Isabella told her. "But I don't really need it. I can wear a T-shirt and shorts over my suit."

She put it back on the rack and kept browsing. She still had a few more days here. The sundress would be nice for dinner tonight, but she should probably get a few more nice things to wear before the week was over. She went over to the shirts and picked out a pale coral shirt with white stripes. It had an open back with a big white bow across the open area.

"That's very nautical," Grandma remarked. "Very nice."

The next shirt she found was ocean blue with a white lace pattern in the front that reminded her of some of the

Native American patterns she had seen in the museum. She picked that one off the rack too.

"I should probably get a pair of shorts," Isabella said thoughtfully.

"How about a skirt?" Grandma asked. She held up a short blue skirt with cute pleats in the front. "This color would go with both the shirts you picked, I think."

"Grandma, it's perfect!" Isabella cried. She took the hanger from her grandmother. "And it's my size! You are a genius!"

"Now, why don't you go try some things on?" Grandma asked.

A salesclerk helped Isabella into one of the fitting rooms, and she tried on the outfits. First the sundress. It fit perfectly, and the billowy skirt fell right below her knees. She came out and made a silly pose.

"What do you think?" she asked her grandmother.

"Just fabulous!" Grandma Miriam said. She turned to the salesclerk closest to her. "Doesn't my beautiful granddaughter look like a model?"

Isabella blushed. Grandma said that whenever they shopped together.

"Absolutely. She's got the height too," said the clerk,

a woman in her early twenties. Isabella blushed again. It was embarrassing, but kind of nice too.

"Let's see the rest!" Grandma said.

Isabella tried on the skirt with the coral T-shirt first, and Grandma agreed that the two colors looked "just fabulous" together. The blue one was "just perfect" too.

"And the shirts go with my denim shorts too," Isabella said, as she did a runway walk for Grandma down an aisle of the store.

"You're a girl after my own heart, Izzy," Grandma Miriam said. "You know just what you want. No hemming and hawing and taking forever."

"My friend Lilly does that," Isabella says. "It gets sooooo boring."

"And now we have time for some more fun before lunch," Grandma said.

"Like what?" Isabella asked.

Grandma's eyes twinkled. "You'll see."

They paid for the clothes and then left the mall. Grandma stopped in a strip mall a few minutes away and parked in front of Lovely's Nail Salon.

"What are we doing?" Isabella asked.

"What do you think?" Grandma replied with a grin.

A bell on the door tinkled when they went inside. An older woman with blond hair piled on top of her head was polishing a woman's nails at a small table near the front of the shop. She looked up when she heard the bell and broke into a big smile.

"Hey there, Miriam!" she said. "I've got two chairs open for you."

"Thanks, Lovely," Grandma said. "Everyone, this is my granddaughter, Isabella, whom you've heard so much about."

The nail technicians all looked up from their workstations and smiled.

"You get yourself over here, young lady," said a dark-haired woman with friendly brown eyes.

Grandma followed Isabella over to the station.

"Isabella, this is Maria," she said.

Isabella smiled shyly. "Hi."

"Climb on up and take off those flip-flops," Maria instructed.

Isabella climbed up onto the big chair and slid off her flip-flops. Grandma Miriam climbed into the chair next to her.

"Now dip your feet into the water, sweetheart," Maria said.

"Thanks," Isabella said. "I've never had a pedicure before."

Maria laughed. "Wait, are you really Miriam's granddaughter? She's in here every week."

"Of course she's Miriam's granddaughter. She looks just like her pictures," said the woman next to her.

"She looks prettier than her pictures," said Lovely, walking over to them. "Isabella, it's such a pleasure to meet you. Your grandma goes on and on about you."

"Thanks. Nice to meet you too," Isabella said, flashing her grandma a smile.

Maria suddenly frowned. "Look at this. There was so much excitement when you came in that I forgot to tell you to pick out a color."

Grandma Miriam handed Maria a bottle of light blue polish. "I picked one out for her. All the young girls are wearing it. And it'll go nice with those new outfits we bought, Izzy."

Lovely shook her head. "Let the girl pick out her own color, Miriam!"

"No, it's okay," Isabella said. "It's pretty."

"So," Maria said as she began to shape Isabella's toenails with a file. "How was your holiday dance recital?"

Isabella was surprised. "You know about that?"

Maria nodded. "Your grandma tells us everything."

Isabella couldn't stop looking at her toes when they left Lovely's shop. They looked prettier than she had ever seen them. She started to walk toward the car, but Grandma stopped her.

"They have the best Arnold Palmers here," she said, nodding to one of the shops in the strip mall. The sign above the door read THE SUNSHINE CAFÉ. Little white tables with orange umbrellas were scattered outside.

"What's an Arnold Palmer?" Isabella asked.

"Delicious, that's what!" Grandma Miriam replied.

Curious, Isabella followed her grandmother inside and watched her order two Arnold Palmers for them. The guy at the counter handed her two tall drinks in clear plastic cups.

"Grab some straws," Grandma said, marching outside.

They sat down under one of the umbrellas. A small breeze was rippling through the air, making it pleasant to be out in the heat. Grandma planted one of the cups in front of her.

"Guess!" she said.

Isabella slipped in her straw and took a sip of the icy cold drink.

"It's kind of like iced tea," she said. "Only lemony and sweet."

"It's half iced tea and half lemonade!" Grandma cried. "Isn't it wonderful?"

Isabella nodded, taking another sip. "It's awesome," she agreed. "Not too sweet like lemonade, and it doesn't have that aftertaste that iced tea has."

Grandma nodded. "Exactly! And they make it the best here."

They sat back and watched the leaves waving on the palm trees around them, quiet for a moment.

"It's so nice to have company!" Grandma sighed, breaking the silence.

For the first time, Isabella wondered if her grandmother was a little lonely down here. She always seemed to be busy, but Isabella knew she did a lot of stuff by herself. The Clarks were all in Chicago, and since Mom was an only child, it wasn't like there were aunts or uncles who could visit.

"You know your mother and I used to go to tea every week!" said Grandma.

Isabella nodded. "She told me. She said you both used to get all dressed up and you would take her to tea at a fancy hotel in downtown Chicago. That must have been nice."

"It was," Grandma agreed.

Dr. Clark worked on most Saturday mornings, and the rest of the weekend they were usually running around to practices and stuff like that. Isabella couldn't imagine either of them having time to get dressed up and have a fancy tea.

"Well, this isn't fancy, but it's tea," Isabella said, and Grandma grinned and held up her cup.

"Cheers, to a beautiful morning with my granddaughter."

Isabella tapped her cup. It was nice being alone with Grandma Miriam. In the past, Jake or her mom had always been with them.

"I wish you lived closer, Grandma," Isabella said.

"Sometimes I do too," she said with a smile. "But I'm glad you're here right now. You can come visit me anytime."

CRUSH

Isabella thought about how disappointed she had been when Mom had announced they were spending spring break here. What had she been thinking? Sure, having Ryan around was a nice bonus. But when it came down to it, it was just nice spending time with Grandma.

chapter 7

GRANDMA STOPPED AT A HOAGIE SHOP AND PICKED
up sandwiches for everyone. While she waited for her
order, she called Rose.

"Bring the boys over to my house in five minutes,"
she said. "I have lunch for us."

Isabella heard Rose say something on the other end,
and then Grandma said, "Yes, you too! I can buy my
friend a sandwich if I want to. And the walk will do you
good."

When they got back to Grandma's condo, Jake and
Ryan were goofing around outside, waiting for them.
Rose was shuffling down the street.

"Yoo-hoo!" She waved.

"Perfect timing, Rose!" Grandma yelled back. "Now,
come on in and eat!"

The boys dug into the bag of hoagies like hungry

wolves and ate their sandwiches in seconds.

"Are you boys ready for the pool?" Grandma asked.

"I've got my suit on," Ryan reported.

"I just need to change," Jake said, darting away from the table.

"Jake! Clear your place first," Grandma scolded.

"Sorry, Grandma." Jake quickly obeyed and went upstairs.

"So how was shopping?" Rose asked.

"Really good," replied Isabella. "I got a new dress to wear tonight."

"I made our reservation for four thirty, so I need you all back from the pool early today," Rose said. "You hear that, Ryan?"

Ryan nodded. "Yes, Gran."

Isabella rose from the table. "I should put away the stuff I got and get on my suit. I'll be right down."

Isabella brought her bags upstairs and noticed that there was one more bag than there should have been. She looked inside and saw the cover-up she had been admiring. She quickly ran downstairs.

"Grandma, thank you! You didn't have to do that!"

"I'm a grandmother. I'm allowed to spoil my grand-children," Grandma replied.

Jake raced past Isabella on the stairs. "What about me? When do I get spoiled?"

Grandma held up a wrapped sandwich. "That's why I got you an extra hoagie."

Jake's eyes lit up. "You're the best!"

Isabella put on her bathing suit, pulled the cover-up over it, and then checked herself out in the mirror. It looked casual but not boring. Perfect! She slid on some flip-flops and headed downstairs. Then she gave Grandma a big hug.

"Thank you so much. It's perfect!"

Jake glanced at her. "Why are you wearing a dress to go to the pool?"

"Jake, you know nothing about fashion," Rose said. "It's a cover-up, and she looks adorable. Doesn't she look adorable, Ryan?"

Ryan blushed and stammered, "Yes, uh, I mean, I guess so."

"I think she looks great."

It was Andrew. He and Ashley had come in through the unlocked front door without knocking. Isabella blushed. Why had Andrew said that in front of everybody?

Then Ashley made things worse.

"That was a fun double date last night," she said, grinning at Jake.

"It was *not* a double date," Isabella said, annoyed—and probably too loudly. Embarrassed, she fled to the bathroom. "I have to put my sunscreen on."

"Everybody needs to put sunscreen on," Grandma Miriam told the others.

When everyone was properly sunscreened, they headed to the pool. Isabella ignored Jake's "Last one in is a rotten egg!" cry and marched to a lounge chair far from the others. She lay down on it, closing her eyes.

Double date? She looks great? Why do those Shelby twins spoil everything? she wondered.

She got bored pretty quickly, and the sound of the kids having fun in the pool was tempting. She looked at her phone and saw two texts from her mom. As she answered them, she spotted Mr. Stern sleeping just a few chairs away.

She quickly snapped a photo of him and sent it to Amanda.

Here's my view at the pool, she typed.

OMG! He's orange! Amanda texted back.

:-P

Where is cute boy? Amanda asked.

Still here.

More pics!

Isabella knew she couldn't just take pictures of Ryan without it looking weird. She got up and walked to the pool.

"Hey, everybody, get together!" she called out. "I need to take a picture for my friend Amanda."

Everyone in the pool obeyed. Andrew made a silly face, and Ashley started splashing Ryan, and then he and Jake splashed her back. Isabella took some pictures and sent them to Amanda.

Who's the blond? Amanda asked.

Ashley.

No, I mean the boy.

Andrew. Her twin bro.

He's cute 2!

Yes, Isabella started to text. She wanted to say, "But he's really annoying," but before she could type, Andrew swam up to the end of the pool and started splashing her.

"Hey, I'm on the phone!" she yelled, blocking her face with her hand.

But Andrew kept splashing.

"I'll stop when you get in the pool!" he yelled back, grinning.

Sighing, Isabella set down her phone on the table, got up, and jumped into the water. Andrew was still splashing her.

"Hey, you said you'd stop if I got in!" she complained.

"Oh, right," Andrew said, putting his hands at his sides.

Isabella smiled wickedly and started splashing Andrew.

"Ha! Got you!" she crowed.

Jake jumped between them. "Splash fight!"

"You kids stop splashing like that!" yelled Mr. Stern, who had woken up from his nap.

Giggling, Isabella stopped splashing. She dove under the water and swam to the other end of the pool without coming up once for air until she reached the end.

As she shook the water out of her ears, she heard Ashley's voice outside the pool.

"I knew it!"

Isabella looked up. Ashley was holding her phone and looking at the screen.

"I knew you had a crush on my brother," she said.

Isabella was horrified. She climbed out of the pool and grabbed the phone from Ashley. "What are you doing?"

"I just wanted to see the pictures," Ashley protested.

Isabella glanced back in the pool. Andrew was smiling like crazy, and Ryan was swimming in the opposite direction.

Is he mad? she wondered. She turned back to Ashley. "You shouldn't have read my texts. That's like reading someone's e-mail."

"Hey, it was right up on the screen," Ashley said. "Relax."

Then she must have seen how angry Isabella was. "I'm sorry," she said. "I guess I shouldn't have read that. Or said that. But it really was right there."

Isabella couldn't even speak. She put on her cover-up, grabbed her towel, and headed back to Grandma's condo.

She heard Ashley, Jake, and Andrew calling after her, but she kept walking. She did not hear Ryan saying anything.

"Izzy? Everything okay?" Grandma asked as Isabella came inside alone.

"I just don't feel like swimming anymore," Isabella replied glumly. "I'm gonna read in my room, okay?"

"Whatever you want. It's your vacation," Grandma said. But she looked worried.

Isabella stomped up the stairs. Having a crush on Ryan had felt simple and nice. But thanks to the Shelby twins, everything was a confusing mess!

chapter 8

ISABELLA HUNG OUT IN HER ROOM FOR A FEW
hours, lazing around and reading a book. Then she heard
the front door slam, and Jake burst into her room a few
seconds later.

"Grandma says to get ready for dinner," he said.

She had almost forgotten about that! She wasn't
sure if she was in the mood anymore. The Shelby twins
wouldn't be there, at least, but how could she face Ryan
after what had happened?

But she knew there was no backing out. With a mom
as a doctor, she could never fake being sick, and she was
pretty sure Grandma would call Dr. Clark if Isabella tried
it with her. She took a quick shower and toweled her hair
until it was mostly dry. Then she put on the new sundress,
a swipe of lip gloss, and her sandals. *Might as well make
the most of it*, she thought.

"What a vision!" Grandma Miriam exclaimed as Isabella came down the stairs. "Izzy, it looks even nicer than it did in the store."

Isabella laughed. "Grandma, it's the same dress!"

Jake came into the room, wearing khaki shorts and a blue short-sleeved shirt with a collar. "Hey, Bella's not the only gorgeous one in this family."

Grandma hugged him. "You! You're so handsome I can't stand it!"

Rose didn't like to drive, so they picked up Rose and Ryan, and Grandma drove to the restaurant. Isabella felt weird in the car, but Ryan and Jake talked the whole time like nothing could possibly be wrong or different. The building the restaurant was in was round, like a sports stadium, only smaller. A giant baseball and bat were over the front entrance.

"Is this a restaurant?" Isabella asked.

"It's owned by Brock Lowry," Ryan explained. "He was a big player in the seventies. There's awesome baseball stuff inside, and the food's really good."

"We always come here when my Ryan visits," Rose said lovingly.

It wasn't crowded inside (probably because it was so

early, Isabella thought), and they got a table with a great view of a giant TV screen. A baseball game was playing on the screen, and from the look and sound of it, Isabella guessed it was an old one. But she was glad something was on the screen, because it gave her an excuse to stare off into the distance. Ryan was sitting right next to her, and it still felt awkward talking to him, even if he was acting like everything was normal.

Grandma handed her a menu, and Isabella accepted it without her usual "thank you."

"Izzy, sweetie, I have to ask," Grandma said gently, whispering. "Is something bothering you?" Because it was Grandma, she didn't exactly whisper, and everyone heard. Isabella turned bright red.

Jake answered for her. "Ashley read her texts or something."

"She *mis*read my texts," Isabella said. "And anyway, it was none of her business."

Grandma quickly changed the subject. "So, Ryan, you really love baseball, don't you? Just like my Jake."

Ryan's face clouded a little.

"He's still upset about those tryouts," Rose offered.

Ryan made a face. "Everyone thought I was a shoo-in,

but I just had a terrible game at tryouts," he admitted. "I got all nervous and distracted."

"I know how you feel," Isabella blurted out. "This fall I had a piano recital. I practiced the same piece for, like, months and months, and I knew it perfectly. Then, the night of the recital, I was really nervous, so I stared at my keys. When I was almost through, I looked up. There were all these faces looking at me! I totally panicked. My hand slipped and I landed on a really bad note and flubbed the rest of the way."

"That's awful," Ryan said sympathetically.

Isabella nodded. "It gets worse. My teacher actually made me start over again! I got it right, but I could tell everyone was feeling sorry for me."

"Nobody noticed," Jake said.

"You're just being nice," Isabella told him. "You played your piece perfectly. Honestly, sometimes I can't believe we're twins!"

That conversation cleared whatever awkwardness was hanging between Isabella and Ryan, and Isabella was able to really enjoy dinner. Ryan told her to order the Home-Run Chicken, which she did, and it was delicious. Then the grandmas even let them order dessert:

an Extra-Innings Sundae with the works. Big scoops of vanilla ice cream dripping with hot fudge and piled high with toasted peanuts, caramel corn, and whipped cream. Everyone got a spoon with an extra-long handle, and they all dug in.

"This was a great idea," Isabella said, taking another spoonful of sundae.

"Oh, and I have good news," Grandma said. "We have something exciting planned for tomorrow. We're going to Adventure Land!"

"No way!" Jake and Isabella cried at once, and Ryan shook his head.

"See? You guys are such twins. You're always saying the same stuff at the same time," he said.

"Not always," Jake and Isabella said together, and everyone cracked up.

"Anyway, I can't believe we're going," Isabella said. She turned to Ryan. "We always ask to go when we're down here, but Dad hates the crowds at amusement parks and Mom thinks it's well . . . too much." She glanced at Grandma Miriam.

"I know I'm an old lady, but I can take you to an amusement park," Grandma Miriam protested. "You twins are old enough to go on rides by yourselves now anyway, as long as you stick with the other kids."

"Other kids?" Isabella's heart sank a little. She had a feeling she knew what was coming.

Grandma nodded. "Yes, the Shelby twins are going. It was their idea!"

Isabella frowned, and she noticed that Ryan didn't look too happy either. But Jake was grinning.

"Awesome! This is going to be great!"

"We're going to go later in the day to avoid the strongest rays of the sun," Grandma told him. "Rose will be staying here, but Lorraine is going to come with us."

"Sounds like fun," Isabella said in a flat voice.

When they got back to Grandma's condo, Isabella was relieved to see that Ashley and Andrew weren't waiting for them like lions ready to pounce on prey. To be sure, she hurried up to her room and closed the door.

You there? she texted Amanda.

☺Amanda texted back.

I need 2 tell you something, Isabella began, and her

fingers flew as she told Amanda about everything—how Ashley read her texts and now Ryan thought she liked Andrew and Andrew liked her and it was so confusing!

Ur lucky! Amanda texted back. U have 2 guys who like u. There are no cute guys here. Just little kids.☹

It's not like that, Isabella typed, but then she paused.

Or was it? It was true. Andrew liked her. She was pretty sure Ryan did too. Yes, it was confusing, but it was still kind of fun. Way more fun than working in her dad's accounting office, for sure.

Ur right, Isabella typed back. I am lucky.

Need details! Amanda demanded.

Promise!

Isabella leaned back on her bed. She wasn't sure what was going to happen at the amusement park tomorrow, but she was pretty sure it was going to be interesting!

chapter 9

"YOU'VE GOT TO RIDE THE STOMACH CHURNER!"
Andrew was saying. "It's killer. There are these three
loops and then this gigantic drop at the end."

Isabella shuddered. "That sounds scary, but fun!"

The next day, the two sets of twins, Ryan,
Grandma Miriam, and Lorraine Shelby stuffed themselves into Lorraine's minivan. Isabella had found herself squeezed between Andrew and Jake in the very
back seat. Ashley and Ryan sat in front of them. She
would rather have Ryan at her side than Andrew, but
at least she wasn't sitting near Ashley. She still got
mad every time she thought about Ashley picking up
her phone.

That left her stuck with Andrew, who had been talking nonstop about every ride in Adventure Land. Isabella
couldn't hear what Ashley and Ryan were talking about,

but Ashley seemed to be laughing a lot, and Ryan was looking kind of down. Isabella wondered why.

"And then there's the Wheel Whipper, which spins around and around at superspeed. I almost upchucked my slushie," Andrew said.

Isabella laughed. Andrew might be annoying, but he was pretty funny sometimes too.

"I hate those spinny rides," she said. "I like roller coasters best."

"I'll go on it with you, dude!" Jake promised, high-fiving Andrew.

It was almost three o'clock when Lorraine pulled into the parking lot.

"Nobody go running off!" Grandma Miriam said as she jumped out of the car. "Not until we go over a few things."

Isabella thought Grandma looked like a gym teacher today, in her sensible sneakers, gray yoga-style pants, and white T-shirt. The only thing "grandma" about her was her floppy sun hat. She took some papers out of her shoulder bag and handed one to each kid.

"We're not doing all this willy-nilly," she said. "I printed out a map of the park and made an agenda for us. We'll visit one section at a time. You can go off on your own, as long as you stay in your section. Lorraine and I will meet you at a different checkpoint in each section when the time is up. Got it?"

"Grandma, you should have been a military strategist," Jake remarked as he looked at the agenda.

"I was a teacher. Same thing," she replied. "Do you know how many school trips I chaperoned? And we never lost a kid. Not one. Now, let's go have some fun!"

The words "Adventure Land" arched above them in huge red letters arched above them as they entered the park. Grandma and Lorraine bought their tickets, and Isabella looked down at the schedule.

3:30–4:30 Old Time Adventure Land, Grandma had typed.

"Cool! The log flume is there!" Andrew cried, and then sprinted away. Ashley followed him.

Isabella and Jake glanced at Grandma.

"Go!" Grandma urged. "Just meet us over by the ice cream stand at four thirty."

"Have fun!" Lorraine called out in a voice even louder than Grandma's.

The twins ran after Andrew and Ashley, and Ryan

lagged behind them. Andrew skidded to a stop in front of the log flume ride.

"This is awesome!" he cried. "And the line's not so bad."

He raced to get in line. Isabella noticed Ryan looking up at the ride. From where they stood, they could see the last drop of the flume as it came down a waterfall and splashed into a pool of water at the bottom.

"Do you think that's the highest drop?" he asked.

Isabella nodded. "The last one on the flume is always the highest. It's not like a roller coaster."

They caught up to the others. After a few minutes, the ride operator helped them into what looked like a big, hollowed-out log with three seats that fit two people each.

Ashley grabbed Ryan's arm and pulled him into the front seat.

"It's the best one!" she yelled.

Jake jumped into the backseat. "No way! You get splashed way more back here."

Andrew grinned at Isabella and waved his arm toward the middle seat. "After you," he said, and Isabella didn't feel like she could refuse. She sighed. She hoped she wouldn't be paired with Andrew the whole time.

The ride operators made sure they were strapped in,

and then the ride started. It sped up and down hills and around corners. Water splashed up at every turn. Then the log pitched down the last steep hill. When they hit the bottom, water splashed up, drenching them all.

"I am soaked!" Isabella said. She laughed as she climbed out of the log.

"We'll dry up in minutes in this heat," Jake promised.

Her brother was right. They waited in line for a roller coaster ride with cars that looked like mine carts, and by the time they got on, their clothes were just about dry. This time, Ryan got in the last seat in the mine cart and motioned for Isabella to sit with him. She quickly slid in next to him. Ashley didn't look upset; she took the front seat again, and Jake joined her this time. Andrew had the middle seat to himself and spread his arms out wide.

"Ah, this is the life!" he said.

The mine cart ride was pretty tame, as far as roller coasters went, but Isabella screamed the whole time anyway. She glanced over at Ryan at one point and noticed his eyes were closed.

Is he afraid? Isabella wondered for a second, but the ride quickly tore up a steep hill, jolting the thought from her mind.

When the ride ended, Ryan's face looked practically green.

"You okay?" Isabella asked him.

"Yeah, fine," Ryan replied. They all walked down the ramp that led off the ride, and Ryan pointed in front of them.

"Let's do the Shooting Gallery," he suggested, and nobody objected. It looked like an Old West shooting gallery in a saloon, with an animatronic man playing piano and lots of root beer bottles on the wall. Most objects in the scene had targets behind them, and you could shoot at them with lasers. When you hit a target, bells or whistles went off or the objects moved around.

By the time they finished playing, it was time to meet the grandmas by the ice-cream stand. Grandma Miriam was looking at her watch as the kids ran up.

"Perfect timing!" she said approvingly. "Next we're going to High-Octave Adventure Land. But first, how about some ice cream?"

"Yes!"

"Yeah!"

"Woo-hoo!"

"It's my treat," Lorraine said, as she purchased an

ice-cream pop for each of them. They thanked Lorraine and happily ate them as they walked to the next area of the park.

The next few hours were a whirlwind. They went on more roller coasters and the Ferris wheel and bumper cars, and Isabella even agreed to go on one spinning ride that didn't look too fast. They ate hot dogs and hot pretzels, and by the time they met up with the grandmas at the final stop, Isabella was exhausted.

"Gran, do we have to go?" Andrew asked Lorraine.

"Your old grandma is getting tired," she said with a grin.

"But I need to do something first," Andrew said. "I'll be fast. Promise. It's right over there." He pointed to one of the carnival games.

"All right. But don't be too long," Lorraine told him.

Andrew darted toward the stand, and everyone else followed him, curious. It was one of those games where you threw darts at balloons to win a prize. Giant stuffed animals hung from the ceiling, and smaller shelves filled with tiny stuffed animals lined the floor under the balloons. A sign on the stand read HIT ANY RED STAR TO WIN A BIG PRIZE.

Andrew gave money to the young man behind the stand and got three darts in return. He closed one eye, aimed carefully, and threw the dart at the balloons.

Pop! The first one hit a green balloon, but there was no star on the wall behind it. The second one didn't hit anything. Then he threw the third . . .

Pop! The dart broke a pink balloon and revealed a red star underneath.

"Woo-hoo!" Andrew cried.

Everyone clapped and cheered for Andrew. Only the guy working the stand seemed unimpressed.

"Which one do you want?" he asked.

"That one," Andrew said, pointing to a giant pink teddy bear with a goofy grin on its face.

That's a funny thing for a guy to pick, Isabella thought—but in the next moment she realized why he had picked it. Andrew handed it right to her!

"Here you go, Isabella," he said as everyone watched.

Isabella was sure she turned as pink as the bear. The thing was half her size.

"Um, thanks," she said, feeling more awkward than she ever had before. This even beat the wrecked piano recital.

"Well, isn't that nice," Grandma Miriam said, raising an eyebrow curiously.

"That's my grandson. He's a sweetheart," Lorraine said proudly.

Ashley appeared holding a snow cone. She thrust it in front of Ryan. "This is for you," she said.

"Um, thanks," Ryan said, echoing Isabella, and now it was Isabella's turn to raise an eyebrow. Ashley had been trying to get close to Ryan all day. *Does she like him now? I thought she liked Jake*, Isabella thought.

"See? My Ashley's a sweetheart too," Lorraine said.

The sky was dark overhead as they walked back to the parking lot.

"So, did you go on any rides, Grandma?" Isabella asked.

"Lorraine and I went on the carousel," Grandma Miriam replied. "And the train ride."

"You need to go on a roller coaster, Grandma!" Jake said.

"Not those loop-dee-loop ones," she said, shaking her head.

They were walking back through Old Time Adventure Land again. Isabella nodded toward the mine cart coaster.

"That one has no loops, Grandma. It's really fun."

"Well, I suppose," Grandma said slowly. "Should we all go on one last ride?"

"I need to finish my snow cone," Ryan said. "And I can hold the teddy bear. But you guys can go on."

Grandma frowned. "You shouldn't be alone. Everyone should have a buddy at all times."

"I'll be his buddy!" Ashley offered, and Isabella tried not to grimace openly.

But she was more excited about going on a ride with Grandma. She, Jake, and Grandma got a cart to themselves. Isabella sat next to Grandma. Andrew and Lorraine had a cart to themselves, too, right in front of them.

The mine cart ride started, and the carts *clicked-clicked-clicked* up the first hill. Then . . . *whoosh!* They fell down the first drop.

"Woooo!" Grandma cried, holding her hands up in the air. Isabella had never seen such a look on her grandmother's face—wild, crazy, and free.

They were all laughing when the carts came to a stop.

"That was fun," Grandma Miriam said. "Maybe next time you come, I'll go on more rides."

Isabella beamed at her grandmother. "I hope we can

spend every spring break with you," she said.

Grandma hugged her. "Me too, Izzy. Me too."

The ride home was quiet, and Isabella dozed off for part of it. She woke up when Lorraine pulled into her driveway.

"Thank you so much for driving, Lorraine," Grandma Miriam said. She nodded to Isabella and Jake. "Why don't you two walk Ryan home?"

"Sure thing, Grandma," Jake said.

Isabella was relieved. She wanted to get away fast from Andrew. She didn't know what to make of the teddy bear. Everyone had joked on the way home that it took up an entire seat.

Isabella, Jake, and Ryan waved good-bye to Ashley and Andrew and headed down the street. When they got to Rose's town house, she was standing at the front door.

"Miriam told me you were on your way," Rose said. "Did you have fun?"

"Lots," Isabella replied. "We went on all the rides."

Rose looked surprised. "But Ryan hates rides! He's afraid of roller coasters."

"Grandma!" Ryan sounded mortified. "Maybe when I was a little kid. But not now."

Isabella remembered how miserable Ryan had looked when he'd heard they were going to Adventure Land, how green he'd looked after he got off the mine carts, and how he kept suggesting they do stuff that didn't involve rides. It all made sense now.

"Ryan! Why did you go on the rides if you don't like them?" Isabella asked.

He shrugged. "I just wanted to hang out with you . . . guys," he replied. Then he gave her a sly smile.

Isabella felt a little flutter of happiness inside her. *Did he do that for me?* she wondered. It sure seemed that way.

"Well, good night," she said, and then she and Jake headed back to Grandma's. When they got there, they found the pink bear sitting comfortably in a chair in her living room.

"You're going to need another seat on the plane for him," Grandma joked as they came in.

"Oh my gosh, I didn't think of that!" Isabella said.

"Don't worry. You can keep it here and see it when you come back to visit."

"Thanks," Isabella said, hugging her.

As she walked up to her room, it hit her. They were

flying home on Saturday morning! They had only two more full days of spring break. And when it was over, she would go back to Chicago and Ryan would go back to New York.

Even if the Shelbys hadn't ruined everything, it wouldn't matter, she thought with a sigh. *What's the point of having a crush on someone I'll never see again?*

THE NEXT MORNING, ISABELLA AND JAKE WERE
sitting at the kitchen table, about to eat breakfast with
Grandma, when there was a knock on the door. Jake ran
to open it. Isabella craned to see who it was. Could it be
Ryan?

"Who wants doughnuts?" Andrew asked, thrusting a
white box at Jake.

Ashley slipped past him. "Gran has another headache," she reported. "She said yesterday was too much
for her."

"Well, it's very nice of you to bring doughnuts for us,"
Grandma Miriam remarked. "Come eat with us. I made
enough scrambled eggs for an army."

Isabella tried not to sigh loudly as Ashley and Andrew
sat down. Even though yesterday had been fun, she was
feeling pretty tired of the twins. Ashley buying Ryan

that snow cone—what was that all about, anyway? And getting that pink teddy bear from Andrew had been so embarrassing!

After they finished eating, Ashley jumped up from the table and grabbed Isabella by the arm. "Come on. I want to see your room," she said.

Ugh, Isabella thought. *How pushy*. "I need to help Grandma clear the table," she said.

"That's okay, Izzy. I've got it. You two have fun," Grandma Miriam said with a wave of her hand.

Andrew started cracking up. "Izzy? Dizzy Izzy! That is great!"

Isabella turned to Andrew and gave him a look that could have disintegrated him.

"Grandma Miriam is the only one who calls me Izzy. The *only* one," she repeated.

Andrew held up both hands. "Whoa, chill out. I got it."

She stomped up the stairs, followed by Ashley. She pushed open the door to the room and flopped on the bed.

"Wow, this room is nice," Ashley remarked as she looked around. "Gran sticks Andrew and me in a room the size of a broom closet. She uses the other guest room for all her clothes and stuff."

"Usually my parents stay in here, and Jake and I have the smaller room too," Isabella told her. "This is a lot better."

Ashley started opening the dresser drawers. "This is such a cute shirt!" she cried, holding up the new blue shirt Isabella had bought the other day. "Why haven't you worn it yet?"

"I thought I'd save it for my last day," Isabella said, eyeing her. Who just opened drawers that weren't theirs? This girl had no boundaries. "In case we do something special. We're leaving the day after tomorrow."

"Yeah, my mom's picking us up later today," Ashley said. "I know you'll miss us. Especially Andrew." She wiggled her eyebrows at Isabella.

It was too much for Isabella. "Listen, mind your own business, okay?" she said. "I don't like Andrew at all. Not. One. Bit."

Ashley didn't seem fazed by Isabella's angry tone. "Well, I read your texts. You like somebody. I know."

"Ryan!" Isabella blurted out, although she had no idea why she was confiding that to Ashley. "I like Ryan, okay?"

Ashley made a face. "You like Ryan? Really?"

Confused, Isabella said, "I thought you liked him too. You bought him a snow cone yesterday."

"I was just trying to make Jake jealous," Ashley confessed.

"I thought you liked Jake!" Isabella cried.

Ashley went to the door and closed it. "Um, yeah, but you don't have to announce it to the world."

Isabella was so angry. This was the girl who had read her texts and gone through her drawers and she wanted her to be quiet about liking her brother. Then it hit her: She liked her brother.

Isabella tried to process this. It was one thing to guess that Ashley liked Jake, but to hear it from Ashley was kind of weird. It was hard to think about anybody having a crush on her brother. He was just so . . . *Jake*.

Ashley sat on the bed next to Isabella. "Your brother is so nice. You should know! You're his twin. Only I wasn't sure if he liked me back, so I thought maybe if I, like, flirted with Ryan a little, he might get jealous. But he didn't even seem to notice."

"Jake's not like that," Isabella told her. "He's pretty chill. But you know, I think maybe he likes you too. I don't think I've ever seen him talk and laugh that much with a girl before."

"Really?" Ashley's face brightened. "Cool. Anyway, I guess it's okay that you like Ryan. Andrew will be crushed, though. He really, really likes you."

Isabella nodded toward the giant pink bear that Grandma had stashed in the corner of the room. "Yeah, I kind of figured."

They both laughed, and Isabella didn't feel so mad at Ashley anymore. She was pretty fun to be around when she wasn't being annoying. Maybe she just couldn't help being a little . . . much, as Grandma would say.

Ashley gave a little sigh. "It's too bad you guys live so far away," she said, and Isabella was reminded of the fact that she and Ryan lived far away from each other too.

"I know," Ashley said, jumping up. "We can't go to the pool until after lunch, right? Then let's invite Ryan over to play a board game or something. That way we can all hang together."

"Sounds good!" Isabella agreed, and they went downstairs.

"Grandmawe'regoingtoinviteRyanoverandallplayaboa rdgameokay?" Isabella said all in one breath.

"That's a wonderful idea!" Grandma Miriam said. "I'll see what games I have in the closet."

Before long, all five of them were around the kitchen table, playing Monopoly and munching on grapes that Grandma had put out for them. Andrew kept buying houses next to houses that Isabella had put on the board.

"Now we're neighbors," he said every time he did it, wiggling his eyebrows just like Ashley had up in Isabella's room.

Must be a twin thing, Isabella thought. And it was kind of cute, but Isabella still cringed every time he did it. She kept looking over at Ryan to see if he noticed, but it didn't seem to bother him.

Andrew kept it up when they all went to the pool after lunch.

"It's time for the pool ball grand championships!" Jake announced, holding the beach ball in the air. He climbed out of the pool and got on the diving board, still holding the ball. He took a deep breath—and then walked swiftly down the board, jumping hard. He curled up his arms and legs around the beach ball as he jumped. He crashed into the water, making a huge splash that sent water flying in all directions.

Jake emerged from the water, sputtering. "Beach ball cannonball!" he yelled triumphantly. "One hundred points!"

Instinctively, the rest of the kids looked at Mr. Stern. Miraculously, he was snoring loudly. Jake's cannonball jump hadn't woken him.

"And you also get an extra fifty points for not waking Mr. Stern," Ashley said.

"What? What about me?" Mr. Stern asked, as he jerked awake.

Andrew gave him a big smile and a wave. "Hope you're having a nice day, Mr. Stern!"

Mr. Stern mumbled something and closed his eyes again.

Then Andrew took the beach ball from Jake. "My turn!" he said. He climbed out of the pool and got on the diving board. As he jumped, he tossed the ball at Isabella and it bounced off her head. "That's worth a thousand points, because Isabella is priceless!" he said.

"No way," Jake protested. "That was a lame trick. Twenty points."

"Yeah, twenty points," Isabella said. "Okay, my turn."

They goofed around for a while, playing pool ball, and then everyone got out to dry off and reapply their sunscreen. Andrew approached Isabella, holding his phone.

"Can I talk to you?" he asked.

"Um, sure," Isabella said, a little nervously.

Andrew started to walk away from the others, and Isabella followed him.

"So, I was wondering if I could take a picture of you," he said. "Then maybe I could show it to people and tell them you're my girlfriend. You could be my girlfriend whenever you come to Florida, if you want."

Isabella didn't know what to say at first. *This is really hard*, she thought. *I don't want to hurt his feelings. Imagine if I asked Ryan to be my boyfriend and he said no. I'd be crushed.*

"Wow, that's really nice of you to ask," she said. "It's just . . . I'm not allowed to be anybody's girlfriend until I'm older. It's my parents' rule. And anyway, I kind of like someone else."

Why did I say that last part? she wondered. It was like there was something in the Florida sunshine that made her want to tell everyone her deepest secrets! But mostly it was because she just didn't know what to say.

Andrew looked sad; Isabella realized she had never seen him do anything but smile. "That's okay. I understand. I hope whoever he is, he deserves you."

Isabella was touched. What a sweet thing to say. "Well, we can still hang out whenever we come down, right?"

Andrew grinned. "Right. Yeah."

Relieved to see Andrew smiling again, Isabella turned back to join the others. She noticed that Ryan was looking at her. When he saw her watching, he quickly looked away.

Did he hear everything? she wondered nervously.

They went back in the pool and swam for a while, until they heard Lorraine's voice call to them from outside the pool fence.

"Andrew! Ashley! Your mom will be here soon. I need you to come out," she said.

"Sure thing, Gran," Ashley said.

She gave Isabella a hug. "Have a safe trip home."

"Give Jake a hug too," she whispered to Ashley. So Ashley gave Jake a hug, and he looked really happy. Then Ashley gave Ryan a quick hug too.

"Bye, Isabella," Andrew said wistfully, giving her a

wave. "Bye, Jake. Bye, Ryan. See you guys around."
Isabella was glad he didn't try to hug her.

She had mixed feelings as she watched them join their
grandmother. On the one hand, it was a relief to see them
go. But on the other hand, the Shelby twins had definitely
made things interesting!

chapter 11

"THROW ON SOME CLOTHES, IZZY!" GRANDMA yelled up the stairs. "Rose is having us over for her famous spaghetti."

"Okay, Grandma!" Isabella yelled back down. She had just showered after their afternoon at the pool. She slipped on a pair of shorts and a T-shirt and brushed out her hair. The sandy brown strands now had golden streaks in them from the sun.

Isabella leaned in to the mirror for a closer look. *It feels like summer*, she thought. The smell of the pool's chlorine still lingered in her nose, and her clothes all smelled like sunshine. She picked up her phone and tapped the screen to get to her weather app. It was thirty-five degrees in Chicago, with an 80 percent chance of sleet. Isabella thought of going back there in two days and shivered.

She came downstairs and found Jake, already dressed,

waiting in the living room with their grandmother.

"Finally!" Jake cried. "I'm so hungry!"

"You ate, like, six bananas and a bag of chips at the pool," Isabella accused.

"It's the Florida sunshine," Jake protested. "It makes me hungry."

"So does the Chicago snow," Isabella teased him.

Jake shrugged. "I'm growing."

"Yeah, maybe you'll catch up to me soon," Isabella teased.

Jake lunged for her, and Isabella darted away. "You are only half an inch taller! And I still say it's because you got measured in your boots last time."

"Did not!" Isabella protested, shrieking.

Grandma Miriam shook her head, smiling. "All right, calm down," she said. "Although I'm glad to see that you two are still young enough to fool around like that. It does my heart good."

Isabella stopped next to Grandma, panting. "Truce," she said, holding out her hand to stop Jake.

Her brother skidded to a halt. "Fine. But when we get back to Chicago, I'm measuring myself again."

Grandma looked at her watch. "It's four thirty-one.

Rose is probably getting anxious. We'd better go."

The big orange sun hung low in the sky as they walked to Rose's condo. Ryan greeted them at the door.

"Grandma's got the table all set," he said, rolling his eyes at Isabella and Jake so that Grandma Miriam couldn't see. "She's dying to eat."

"That's good, because I'm starving!" Jake said, and he jogged into the kitchen, where Rose was sitting at the table.

"Finally!" she said. "Come, eat before it gets cold."

As soon as they sat down, she passed around a big bowl of spaghetti.

"So do you guys play lacrosse?" Ryan asked, as they started to dig into their food. "I just got an e-mail about tryouts for the summer league. I can't wait. I only started playing a year ago, but I think it's even more fun than baseball."

"I played when I was in elementary school," Isabella said. "It was fun, but I like soccer better. Jake plays, though."

"Yeah, I played in the summer league last year," Jake said, his mouth full of spaghetti.

"It's a traveling league," Ryan went on. "I really hope

I make the team. There's a big national meet every year that's really cool."

Jake nodded excitedly. "Our team went to the national meet last year. This year it's outside of Chicago. You should totally come stay with us."

At this, Isabella's ears perked up. *Game changer*, she thought. Here she had been thinking that she might never see Ryan again unless they both happened to be visiting their grandmas at the same time.

"That would be great," Ryan said, looking at Jake. "That would be cool if our teams got to play against each other."

Grandma Miriam looked at Jake and Isabella. "I can't believe tomorrow is your last day here before you fly out. I'm going to miss you two. I kind of got used to having you here."

"I feel the same way about Ryan," Rose said sadly. "It gets so lonely here sometimes."

"That's why we all need to go out for a fancy dinner tomorrow night!" Grandma Miriam said. "We'll make it a day to remember. So I was thinking maybe we could do the beach tomorrow too."

"Really?" Isabella had been having so much fun at the

pool that she had forgotten all about the beach.

Grandma Miriam nodded. "Only if we leave early. And we'll rent one of those big umbrellas at the beach. And wear lots of sunscreen."

"Yes, yes, and yes!" Isabella and Jake said together, and Ryan laughed.

"Twins," he said, shaking his head.

"Ryan, would you like to come too?" Grandma asked.

Ryan looked at his grandmother. "Can I?"

Rose sighed. "Of course. I'll miss you, though."

"We won't be all day," Grandma Miriam promised. "And then we'll all go out to eat. You'll get plenty of Ryan time. I promise."

Plenty of Ryan time. That sounded good to Isabella too.

After dinner, they all watched TV for a little while, and then Jake and Isabella headed home with Grandma Miriam.

"Big day tomorrow," she said, telling them to get ready for bed, and Isabella hadn't objected. As much fun as it had been to hang out with Ryan, she was tired after another long day.

The phone rang, and Jake ran and grabbed it.

"Hey, Mom," he said.

Restless as always, Jake roamed the first floor as he talked to their mom. Isabella waited patiently for her turn to talk. Finally he handed her the phone.

"So Jake was telling me about your new friend Ryan," Mom said. "He asked me if Ryan could stay with us during the lacrosse meet. What's he like?"

"Oh!" Isabella replied. "He's *so* cute and really nice, and he is smart, and . . ."

She realized she was babbling and was relieved when her mom interrupted her, laughing. "He sounds great. I'm glad you'll get to see him again."

Mom had a lot to say about what to do at the airport Saturday before she ended the call. Isabella hung up the phone, thinking.

Ryan had said he was excited to come to Chicago and maybe play against Jake's team. He hadn't really said anything about seeing Isabella. *It wasn't like he needed to say anything*, she thought, *but what if he just wants to see Jake? I thought he liked me back, but maybe I've been wrong this whole time.*

She wasn't sure why, but the thought that Ryan didn't like her back latched on to her brain and wouldn't let go. Had she been reading everything wrong this whole time? And if he *didn't* like her back, he had heard her tell Andrew that she liked someone else. Maybe he knew she liked him and he didn't like her. How embarrassing!

The thought kept her from falling asleep that night. She looked at the digital clock—it was 10:05, and she didn't feel sleepy at all. She thought about reading a book, but she had left it downstairs.

Might as well get it, she thought. Reading always helped her fall asleep.

She tiptoed downstairs and found Grandma Miriam watching TV and eating a big bowl of ice cream.

"Grandma!" Isabella said, surprised.

"What?" Grandma said. "I'm old enough to do what I want. Sometimes I like ice cream at night. Want some?"

"Of course!" Isabella replied.

She followed Grandma into the kitchen and watched her scoop out a big bowl of chocolate, vanilla, and strawberry ice cream. Then they went back into the living room, and Isabella curled up onto the couch next to Grandma. On the TV, an old mystery show with a white-haired lady detective was playing.

"They don't make shows today like they used to," Grandma Miriam said, shaking her head. "All the reality shows these days. Bleh!"

"Some of them are good," Isabella offered. "I like the ones where they have competitions. Like to see who can bake the best cake."

"Yes, but those dating competitions are awful!" Grandma protested, shaking her head. "I hope you never end up on television looking for someone to marry." She shuddered.

Then she looked at Isabella. "Are you having a good time, sweetie?"

"Oh, yes!" Isabella answered.

"Good," Grandma said with a nod. "Now that you're older, maybe you and Jake can visit more often. I'd like that."

Then she paused. "And maybe Ryan will visit too."

Isabella turned red. *How does Grandma know that I like him?* Then she sighed. "What's the use? First of all, I don't even know that he likes me like that. And second of all, he lives in New York and I live in Chicago!"

"On the first count," said Grandma, "trust me. I've seen how he looks at you. And who could not love my

Isabella? And on the second count," she continued. "Did I ever tell you the story of how Grandpa and I lived apart for a year before we got married?"

Isabella shook her head. "No. Really?"

"A whole year," she replied. "I was only nineteen when Grandpa Ben and I fell in love. I was so happy. But then his family decided to move to Chicago to start up their shoe business there—we were living in Boston at the time. That's where we both grew up."

Isabella nodded. "I think I remember that."

"Well, I was heartbroken," Grandma Miriam continued. "Grandpa told me we'd figure it out. This was way back in the days before the Internet and cell phones. So we wrote letters to each other every week. We talked on the phone when we could afford it. And after a year, Grandpa came back with a ring and asked me to marry him. And the rest, as you know, is history."

She smiled, remembering.

"Grandma, I'm not thinking about marrying Ryan." Isabella giggled.

"Of course you aren't!" said Grandma. "I'm just saying that where there's a will, there's a way."

Isabella thought about this for a bit. "Yes, I guess there is," she said, standing up.

"Do you want to watch the show with me?" Grandma asked.

"That's okay, Grandma," Isabella said. "I'm pretty sleepy now. But thanks for the ice cream. And the talk."

Grandma Miriam smiled. "Anytime, Izzy."

The next morning Grandma woke them up at seven a.m.

"The beach is waiting for us!" she yelled when she opened Isabella's door. "It's your last day here! Let's make it count!"

Isabella jumped out of bed, excited. Grandma's energy was contagious. Isabella wanted to make the most of the day too.

She dressed in her bathing suit and then headed downstairs. Along with cereal boxes, she saw an old wood box on the kitchen table.

"What's this?" asked Jake, who walked in behind her.

"Something Isabella wanted to know about," said Grandma. "Last night I was telling her a story about me and Grandpa Ben."

"What? I don't get stories?" Jake asked, pretending to be hurt.

Grandma told the story to Jake as Isabella opened the box. It was filled with letters addressed to "Miss Miriam Applestein" and "Mr. Ben Stone."

"Oh my gosh!" Isabella said when Grandma had finished her story. "Are these the letters that you and Grandpa sent to each other?"

Grandma nodded. "Every one."

"Can I read one?" Isabella asked.

Grandma looked at the clock. "We have time. The lifeguards don't show up until nine. But let me get you a good one."

Grandma dug through the pile and finally pulled one out. "Here you go, Izzy."

Isabella carefully took the letter out of the envelope.

Dear Miriam,

Business is good here at the shoe store. But the women in Chicago all have much bigger feet than they do in Boston. Not nice ones like yours.
Simon and I saw a double feature last night. Two

Western pictures, but the acting wasn't very good.

Remember when we saw South Pacific at the Rialto? Now, that was a picture! And you are a lot nicer to sit next to than Simon. He smells like frankfurters.

Your last letter made me laugh. Please say hi to Howie for me.

Love,
Ben

Jake laughed. "Big feet in Chicago? Ha! I knew you had big feet, Isabella."

"It's really sweet," Isabella said. "And funny, too. But who were Simon and Howie?"

"Simon was Grandpa's brother, who died before you both were born," Grandma replied. "And Howie was Grandpa's best friend in Boston. Oh, he was a fun one. What good times we had."

She sounded happy, but she had a sad look in her eyes. *She must miss Grandpa a lot*, Isabella realized.

"Come on, Grandma," Isabella said. "The beach is waiting!"

Grandma lived close to the beach, and it didn't take long to get there after they picked up Ryan. By nine o'clock, they were set up under two giant umbrellas, and each lifeguard chair had a guard in it.

"Last one to the water is a rotten egg!" Jake yelled, and Ryan and Isabella ran after him, laughing.

The water was colder than the pool, but Isabella didn't mind. She was in the ocean! In March! The sky was a beautiful, cloudless blue, and the sand sparkled white and clean. It couldn't have been a more perfect day.

They splashed and rode the waves for a while and then, tired out, went back to the umbrellas for a rest. They stretched out on their towels under the shade of the umbrella. The warm sun felt good on Isabella's wet skin.

"Hey, Bella, get your big feet off my towel!" Jake yelled, giving her feet a little push. Isabella scowled at him.

"Will you quit it with the 'big feet' comments?" she said.

Ryan laughed. "You do not have big feet."

"Thank you," Isabella said.

"Grandma Miriam showed us a letter this morning," Jake explained, "from, like, the fifties or something. And my Grandpa Ben worked in a shoe store and said that women in Chicago had big feet."

Ryan laughed again. "He wrote a letter about that?"

"He wrote tons of letters," Jake said. "He lived in Chicago and Grandma lived in Boston, so they wrote letters back and forth."

"Yes, we did," Grandma Miriam piped up, looking up from her book.

"Well, you didn't have text or e-mail or Skype and all that," Jake told her. He turned back to Ryan. "Like, we can text you and stuff after we all go back home. It could be like we live next door."

Isabella smiled into her towel. Texting and Skyping Ryan would be awesome, and now Jake had set the stage for it. She quickly forgave him for the "big feet" comments.

"If not, we'll see each other in August, if I get onto the lacrosse team," Ryan said.

Oh no, Isabella thought. *Does that mean he doesn't want to stay in touch?*

The conversation died down, and all was quiet for a

moment. Then Isabella heard Jake texting busily on his phone. She leaned over to his towel and peeked at his screen.

"You're texting Ashley?" she asked, surprised.

Jake shrugged. "She's funny," he explained, and didn't say anything more. Isabella rolled back over onto her towel.

Jake had seemed unusually curious about the letters. Now she had an idea why. It looked like he was excited about texting and Skyping Ashley!

"DON'T YOU TWO LOOK FABULOUS!" GRANDMA Miriam cried.

Isabella did a twirl, and the skirt she had bought at Sparks fluttered around her. She had paired it with her new blue T-shirt and a green cardigan she had brought from home.

"I wouldn't call it fabulous, but it works," Isabella said.

"Speak for yourself," Jake protested. "I'm definitely fabulous."

Grandma Miriam laughed. "Izzy, hold on. I've got something for you."

She left the living room and came back a minute later holding a small white box.

"This is a present," she said as she handed it to Isabella.

Isabella opened the lid and gasped. Inside was a

heart-shaped silver locket. She had seen it before on Grandma, who had told her that Grandpa Ben had given it to her. Isabella had always loved it. The heart was engraved with a pretty design of a rose with leaves all around it.

"It's for you to have now," Grandma Miriam said, and she took it out of the box and put it around Isabella's neck. Isabella ran to the mirror on the living room wall.

"It looks perfect!" Isabella said. She ran back and hugged Grandma. "Thank you so much!"

"I know you'll take good care of it, Izzy," Grandma said, and when Isabella broke away from the hug, she saw tears in Grandma Miriam's eyes.

"I will. I promise," Isabella said.

They piled into Grandma's car and picked up Rose and Ryan. This time, Isabella got stuck with the middle seat, and Ryan and Jake sat on either side. Like Jake, Ryan had put on khakis and a short-sleeved, collared shirt for the occasion.

"You look nice," she said before she could stop herself.

Ryan grinned at her. "Thanks. So do you guys."

So maybe he had said "guys" at the end, but she was still included in that. Isabella let that roll around in her mind on the ride to the restaurant. It was a nice feeling.

Soon Grandma pulled up in front of the restaurant, which was set on the water, like the seafood place they had gone to earlier in the week. But this one looked much fancier, and Isabella was glad she had worn the skirt.

They got a table out by the water again, and the small breeze from the surface danced across their table.

"They have the best early bird specials here," Rose announced as she picked up the menu. "You get an appetizer and a dessert!"

Isabella ordered Caesar salad for her appetizer and scallops for dinner. Jake ordered alligator nuggets and crabs.

"Seriously? You're going to eat alligator?" Isabella asked him, making a face.

"Ashley dared me to," he said with a shrug, and Isabella and Ryan looked at each other in surprise.

"Well, I'm glad Ashley's not texting me," Ryan said. "I'm having the crab cakes."

When their food came, Jake made a big deal of taking a photo of the alligator nuggets, and then he took another picture of himself eating one. Isabella knew he was texting Ashley.

"Jake, when you're done with that, please put your

phone away," Grandma Miriam said. "We don't need technology to enjoy our meal."

Isabella couldn't stop thinking as she ate her meal. Jake and Ashley were constantly texting each other. If Ryan liked her, why hadn't he asked for her number?

Maybe it's enough that I'll see him in August, she thought, casting a sideways glance at him. *That is, if he makes the team.*

"I bet Mr. Stern is going to miss us," Ryan joked.

"I'm sure he will," Grandma Miriam said. "He's not happy unless he has someone to yell at."

Jake had sucked the meat out of his crab legs and was making them walk across the table. Across from him, Rose was giggling like crazy.

"I can make them do the can-can," Jake said, making the legs do kicks.

Grandma Miriam shook her head. "Oh, you remind me of Ben sometimes. He was always such a cutup."

Jake beamed. "Really? I remind you of Grandpa?"

Grandma Miriam nodded. "He had a good heart. You do too."

"So I have a good heart, and Isabella has big Chicago feet," Jake said.

Isabella stuck her tongue out at him. "Good heart? Did you hear that, Grandma?"

Ryan smiled. "Twins!"

When they left the restaurant, everyone was laughing and talking about the fun things that had happened during the week. The good mood lasted until Grandma Miriam drove into the condo complex. Isabella knew that she and Jake were flying out early in the morning. This was good-bye—and maybe the last time she would ever see or talk to Ryan.

Grandma drove to Rose's house and parked out front. They all got out of the car.

"See you around, man," Ryan said, shaking Jake's hand.

Isabella stood there, feeling awkward. Then Ryan turned to her and gave her a hug! Her heart was beating so fast, but she could feel the eyes of Jake and Grandma and Rose on them, and it made her palms sweat.

"Well, good-bye," Isabella said.

"Yeah," said Ryan.

"Dude, you need to get our numbers in your phone," Jake said, taking out his own phone. "Give me your number. I'll send you mine and Bella's right now, okay?"

"Okay," Ryan replied, and Isabella thought he looked relieved. Had he been too shy to ask on his own? Thank goodness Jake was so friendly!

Still, she was sad when they climbed back in the car and drove to Grandma's house. She was about to go inside when she heard Grandma Miriam behind her.

"What do you know? Rose left her sunglasses in the car," she said. She handed them to Isabella with a twinkle in her eye. "Can you run these over to her for me?"

"Sure," Isabella answered eagerly. She practically skipped down the sidewalk all the way to Rose's. Maybe she'd get to see Ryan again one last time.

Probably Rose will answer the door, she thought, not wanting to get her hopes up.

She took a deep breath and rang the bell. The door creaked open and there was Ryan on the other side. He looked surprised to see her.

Isabella held out the glasses. "Your grandmother left these in the car," she said.

Ryan stepped outside, and Isabella realized it was the first time they had been alone together all week.

"Hey, I've been meaning to talk to you . . ." Ryan sounded a little nervous. "Can we e-mail each other or text or something when we get back? I don't know if I can wait until August to talk to you again."

Isabella beamed. "Of course! Text me anytime."

Ryan hugged her again. When he pulled back, she felt his lips graze her cheek.

"Safe travels, Bella. I'll see you soon!" he said.

"I hope so," she said, smiling back at him.

Feeling giddy, she walked backward until she couldn't see Ryan anymore, and he stayed by the door, waving the whole time. Then she turned and floated all the way back to Grandma Miriam's house.

"How'd it go?" Grandma asked.

"Great," Isabella said with a big grin on her face. "I'm going to go pack."

She went back up to the room and set aside an outfit for the morning. Then she took her suitcase from under her bed and opened it up. She was certain that she could still feel the exact spot where Ryan had kissed her on the cheek. And his words kept repeating in her mind.

I don't know if I can wait until August to talk to you again.

She put down the shirt she was folding and picked up her phone, texting Amanda.

Remember that boy Ryan?

Y! Amanda replied.

He likes me back. <3

Lucky!!!!!!!

"Yes, I am lucky," Isabella whispered out loud.

Grandma Miriam made them go to sleep early and got them up at five the next morning. Isabella yawned the whole way to the airport. Grandma parked and then walked them to their gate.

"Look at you two!" she said. "I think you've each grown two inches this week."

Jake sidled up next to Isabella. "I bet I'm finally taller than you!"

Grandma's eyes were filled with tears. She enclosed both of them in her arms and gave them a big hug.

"I'm going to miss you," she said. "They're giving a Skype class at the library next week. Once I figure out how to do it, you'll be seeing my face again soon, okay?"

"That would be awesome," Isabella said.

Then Grandma Miriam left them with a flight attendant, who led them to the boarding area. This time, Isabella and Jake lounged in the seats there, too tired to walk around. After a few minutes, Isabella's phone started beeping.

"It's Grandma," she told Jake. Then she started typing.

Yes, we got to the boarding area ok.

Her phone beeped again. This time, it was her mom.

Are you guys at the boarding area yet?

Yes!!! Isabella texted back.

She looked at her brother. "They are driving me crazy!"

"They're texting me too," Jake said.

Isabella's phone beeped again. She sighed and looked at the screen.

It was from Ryan!

Thanks for saving spring break. Talk soon . . .

Isabella texted back.☺ ☺

Then she sank back in her seat. *Spring break had been great after all*, she thought. Grandma Miriam was a lot of fun. Florida was really nice. And her vacation was definitely not boring. It wasn't the spring break she'd originally hoped for. It wasn't the spring break she'd expected. It had been a lot better. She smiled as the flight attendants told them to turn off their phones. Who cared if it was snowing in Chicago and there were weeks and weeks before she'd get to wear her new spring clothes? She had Ryan to look forward to. *Now bring on summer.*

ANGELA DARLING was nicknamed "The Love Guru" by her friends in school because she always gave such awesome advice on crushes. And Angela's own first crush worked out pretty well . . . they have been married for almost ten years now! When Angela isn't busy watching romantic comedies, reading romance novels, or dreaming up new stories, she works as an editor in New York City. She knows deep down that *every* story can't possibly have a happy ending, but the incurable romantic in her can't help but always look for the silver lining in every cloud.

Here's a sneak peek at the next book in the series:

Cindy likes Edward.

CR♥SH

Does he like her too?

Cindy's Cruise Crush

"WE'RE HERE!" CINDY LEWIS CRIED. SHE SHIELDED her eyes from the sun as she stared up at *The Princess of the Seas*, a massive cruise ship that would be her home for the next five days. "I can't believe we're *finally* here!"

Cindy's stepsisters, identical twins named Olivia and Sophia, glanced at the ship.

"Yay," Olivia said, sounding bored. "A boat." She started texting someone on her shiny new phone.

"I can't wait to get on board!" Cindy continued. "I mean, just *look* at it! It's—it's amazing!"

"Just amazing?" snickered Sophia. "Not, like, *totally amazing*?"

Olivia glanced up from her phone. "Not *totally the most amazing EVER*?" she added.

Then Olivia and Sophia cracked up as they did their

special double-snap-high-five combo. A few days ago, just before Cindy's dad, Mark, had married the twins' mom, Leslie, Cindy tried to join in their high five.

She hadn't made that mistake again.

Cindy shrugged off the twins' laughter. So maybe she was a little excited about the cruise. *What was wrong with that?* Cindy had dreamed about going on a cruise for as long as she could remember. It seemed so romantic—five dazzling days at sea, four starlit nights, and one exotic port of call on a tropical island. She had practically memorized the brochure her dad had given her when he and Leslie had invited the girls to join them on their honeymoon.

"What do you think, princess?" her dad asked Cindy as he joined the girls. "Pretty swanky, huh?"

"Definitely," Cindy replied, still staring at the ship.

The Princess of the Seas was unlike any boat Cindy had ever seen before. It had sixteen decks, and was taller than all of the buildings in the town where she lived. Each deck was decorated with elaborate carvings and jewel-toned banners that fluttered in the ocean breeze. Garlands of tropical flowers swooped around the railings. The shimmery gold trim against the bright white ship reminded Cindy of a sunburst gleaming through a cloud. Somehow it made the ship look like a magical place. A place where anything could happen. A place where maybe—just maybe—dreams could come true.

The whole weekend had felt like a dream to Cindy. It was hard to believe that just two days ago, her dad and Leslie had gotten married! Cindy would never forget how it felt to walk down the aisle on her father's arm or to stand with Olivia and Sophia as one of Leslie's junior bridesmaids. And when her dad and Leslie shared their first kiss as husband and wife, that moment was so beautiful that happy tears had filled Cindy's hazel eyes. Just remembering it made Cindy grin. She truly felt like the luckiest girl on the planet. Not only were her parents still friendly—Cindy's mom had even attended the wedding—but Leslie seemed like the nicest stepmother ever. And the twins had instantly become Cindy's stepsisters. Cindy had always wanted a sister. And now she had two!

A large crowd had gathered on the dock. Cindy turned to her dad. "Are all these people going on the cruise?" she wondered.

"I don't think so," her dad replied as he scanned the

crowd. "Bon voyage—the moment when the ship sets sail—is a big deal. Lots of people come to wave good-bye to the passengers."

Despite the warmth of the day, Cindy felt a shiver of anticipation when her dad said "bon voyage." It sounded so exciting!

"I can't wait to explore the ship," Cindy said. "When do you think we can board?"

"How about right now?" Leslie asked as she joined them. "All our luggage is ready to be loaded, and I've got our boarding passes right here. So what are we waiting for?"

Then Leslie noticed that Olivia was still glued to her phone. She and Cindy's dad exchanged a glance. "Finish that text, and hand it over," Leslie said, with her palm out. "You too, Sophia."

"And you, princess," Dad said to Cindy.

"But why?" asked Sophia.

"Using a cell phone on a cruise ship is ridiculously expensive," Leslie explained. "I'm talking international roaming charges. Even a short call could cost hundreds of dollars."

"But I won't call anyone," Olivia said, still grasping

her phone. "I'll only use my phone for texting. Promise."

"Texting is just as expensive," Leslie said firmly. "Besides, this is our very first vacation as a family. It's for spending time together, not sending texts."

With a loud sigh, Olivia finally gave up her phone. But she didn't look happy about it.

Leslie led them over to the long ramp that stretched up to the ship. Near the base stood a man who was wearing a funny-looking pinafore, with a long gold trumpet in one hand. He unfolded their boarding passes with a flourish. "Hear ye, hear ye," he announced in a booming British accent. "Presenting the honorable Mr. and Mrs. Lewis!"

"Mrs. Lewis, huh?" Leslie said with a grin. "Sounds good to me. I think I could get used to that."

"You'd better," Cindy's dad replied as he put his arm around her.

"Gag me," Olivia whispered to Sophia.

Cindy pretended that she hadn't heard. She thought it was adorable that her dad and Leslie were so much in love.

"And the fair maidens Lady Olivia, Lady Sophia, and Lady Cindy, of the house of Lewis!" the man continued.

Cindy tried not to giggle as she walked up the ramp. Yes, the whole scene was kind of corny.

But it was kind of fun, too.

"Marshall," Olivia suddenly said, stopping short.

Everyone turned to look at her.

"It's Olivia and Sophia Marshall. Not Lewis," she continued.

The town crier bowed low. "A thousand pardons, milady," he said.

Olivia ignored him as she continued up the ramp.

Cindy flashed an apologetic smile at the town crier as she followed Olivia. *What was Olivia's problem, anyway? It was an honest mistake. Who cared? And why was she acting like it would be the worst thing in the world to have the last name Lewis?*

Just before they reached the top of the ramp, a jester leaped in front of them, making Leslie jump.

"Hark! Who goes there?" he called. "A pair of love-birds, newly wed, about to embark on the sweetest of honeymoons?"

Leslie turned to her husband with her hands on her hips. "Did you tell them it was our honeymoon?" she asked, pretending to be mad.

"Guilty," he said with a grin. "So you'd better get used to the special attention."

"Allow us to capture this moment for posterity," the jester said as he ushered the two of them over to a photographer. The jester made a big show of posing them before a large cardboard castle. "Now say 'Cheese!'"

"Cheese!" they chorused, with enormous smiles on their faces. Then Cindy's dad turned to the photographer. "Can we get a copy of that?"

"Sure," she replied. "There's a photo gallery on B deck. We take pictures of the guests throughout the cruise and hang them there for everyone to see. The photos are also available for purchase."

"And now the whole family!" the jester cried as he brought Cindy, Sophia, and Olivia over to the castle. "Sire, let's have you stand just behind your beautiful daughters with your lady fair beside you."

Olivia whispered something to Sophia, just low enough that Cindy couldn't quite hear it. But from the way Sophia dissolved into giggles, Cindy had a feeling that whatever Olivia had said, it wasn't very nice.

Is this how it's going to be for the whole trip?

Cindy wondered. *Olivia constantly snarking on every-thing. . . and Sophia laughing at her cracks?*

"One . . . two . . . ," the photographer said as she peered into the camera.

Well, let them be that way, Cindy decided. *I've been looking forward to this cruise for months, and I'm going to enjoy it. No matter what.*

"You know, hold on a second," the photographer said. She hurried over to the group and put her hands on Cindy's shoulders. "You're so tall that I'm going to put you right back here next to your dad . . . there . . . that's better."

Cindy flicked her long blonde hair over her shoulder as the photographer returned to the camera. She smiled as big as she could. . . .

And then it happened.

Cindy spotted the cutest boy she had ever seen.

He was walking up the ramp, wearing a sky-blue T-shirt and a pair of cargo shorts. The sun glinted off his reddish-brown hair. He squinted a little in the bright light and stopped for a moment to look at *The Princess of the Seas.* Another guy behind him—his brother, maybe?—gave him a little push. The boy almost stumbled, but he caught himself, laughing. The way his smile reached all the way to his eyes—the way his nose crinkled a little as he laughed—Cindy felt like she could barely breathe. She was dizzy and giddy and all fluttery inside, like a hummingbird carried away on the ocean breeze.

Then the gorgeous guy looked right at Cindy.

And smiled just for her!